P9-DHP-662

CYLON CONTACT

Starbuck's *Viper* disappeared into the void, and then his voice came back:

"Targets!"

Apollo requested further transmission, telling Starbuck to pull back; Starbuck apparently didn't hear, for he said that he was practically on top of them. Then, suddenly:

"I am on top of them!"

There was a long silence filled with static, then his next communication:

"Apollo, I'm in trouble!"

THE TOMBS OF KOBOL
The new space adventure from
the TV spectacular,
BATTLESTAR GALACTICA

Berkley Battlestar Galactica Books

BATTLESTAR GALACTICA
by Glen A. Larson and Robert Thurston

BATTLESTAR GALACTICA 2: THE CYLON DEATH MACHINE
by Glen A. Larson and Robert Thurston

BATTLESTAR GALACTICA 3: THE TOMBS OF KOBOL
by Glen A. Larson and Robert Thurston

BATTLESTAR GALACTICA: THE PHOTOSTORY
by Glen A. Larson
Edited and adapted by Richard J. Anobile

BattlestaR
GALACTICA 3
THE TOMBS OF KOBOL
NOVEL BY
GLEN A. LARSON AND ROBERT THURSTON

Based on the Universal Television Series
"BATTLESTAR GALACTICA"
Created by
GLEN A. LARSON
Adapted from the episode
"Tombs of Kobol"
Written by GLEN A. LARSON
& DONALD BELLISARIO

A BERKLEY BOOK
published by
BERKLEY PUBLISHING CORPORATION

BATTLESTAR GALACTICA 3: THE TOMBS OF KOBOL

A Berkley Book / published by arrangement with
MCA PUBLISHING, A Division of MCA Inc.

PRINTING HISTORY
Berkley edition / September 1979
Second Printing

All rights reserved.
Copyright © 1979 by MCA PUBLISHING, A Division of MCA Inc.
This book may not be reproduced in whole or in part,
by mimeograph or any other means, without permission.
For information address: MCA PUBLISHING, A Division of MCA Inc.
100 Universal City Plaza, Universal City, California 91608.

ISBN: 0-425-04267-7

A BERKLEY BOOK ® TM 757,375
Berkley Books are published by Berkley Publishing Corporation,
200 Madison Avenue, New York, New York 10016.

PRINTED IN THE UNITED STATES OF AMERICA

Battlestar GALACTICA 3
THE TOMBS OF KOBOL

PROLOGUE

Baltar distinctly remembered dying. Yes, he must be dead. The memory was quite vivid. If he opened his eyes now, what would he see? Nothingness? The afterlife? A vast drifting cloud-land where religion was being practiced daily? Or perhaps an eternity of flame and torture? Since he believed devoutly in *all* of these possibilities, he decided to wait a while before opening his eyes.

Instead, he concentrated on recalling the events leading up to his death. The Imperious Leader of the Cylons had suddenly turned against him, reneging on a bargain that the Cylons had themselves originally proposed, a bargain whose lucrative terms had influenced Baltar to dupe his own people by pretending to be an envoy of the peace mission that veiled the actual Cylon invasion of the human race's twelve home worlds. After the Leader had told Baltar he no longer figured in the Cylons' plans, Baltar made a last desperate plea to save himself. However, the Leader merely listened to Baltar's protests passively, then he turned his massive body slightly toward a nearby executive officer and ordered that Baltar be taken away to be beheaded. Baltar knew he made a cowardly sight as the officer dragged him—screaming, squirming, crying—from the command chamber. He shuddered now as he remembered that he had indeed cried. *Real* tears, the first real tears that had fallen from his eyes since his overbearing and aristocratic mother had caught him in one of his earliest betrayals.

The officer had dragged him down several corridors to the execution chamber which was located in the interior abyss of the base star. The executioner had immobilized Baltar's fierce bodily resistance by pressing against a pressure point in his neck and paralyzing his central nervous system. While Baltar lay helpless, the executioner showily tested the fine edge of his long-handled ax, deliberately angling its luminescent metal toward a bright electric torch, sending bright rays of light to pain Baltar's tear-ridden eyes. Satisfied that the blade was honed to its keenest edge, the executioner then raised the circular ax above Baltar's face (Cylons always beheaded with the victim staring up at his executioner) and Baltar closed his eyes. His body would have trembled uncontrollably had it not already been numbed. Above him he heard the whoosh of the ax beginning to fall. Then, nothing. His mind had remained a blank until just now, when consciousness had returned to him in a sudden rush.

Thinking back to the horrifying sound of the ax descending toward his throat, he suddenly remembered an accompanying sound, a gentle underscoring to the brutal melody of the ax. A soft, velvety voice whispering: "Wait." Had he actually heard that? No, his memory must be playing tricks on him. There had been no—

"I sense that you are no longer unconscious. Are you feeling better, Baltar?"

That voice again! Soft, velvety, the same voice that had called wait.

"Must you continue to keep your eyes closed? Or is the sealing of your organs of sight one of those curious and absurd human customs that—"

"I am determined to keep my eyes shut," Baltar whispered. Then he realized the implications of that declaration. His eyes *were* shut. His eyes. On his head. He still had his head! He could not open and close his eyes if—

He opened his eyes.

"Ah, that's better." The soft voice dropped half an octave. "Well, at least marginally."

Baltar, frightened, considered closing his eyes again. He had expected to see a typical Cylon, either a warrior in full regalia or that reptilian sort of beast they became when they rose to second or third brain status. But this creature was a different sort of monster altogether, a glittering, gleaming, tall creature which dazzled the eye with its ornate surfaces and gave off a metallic odor that was stronger and muskier than the normal Cylon battlesuit.

Baltar struggled to focus attention on the individual parts of the creature. Lights flashed incessantly from its transparent bulblike head. Instead of a single red beam drifting back and forth across a helmet, the creature appeared to have *two* red lights smoothly moving counter to each other in a pair of slanted eye-sockets. Its mouth, a narrow slit, was lit from within by some sort of phosphorescent blue illumination. Tall and slim, it held its gloved hands primly in front of its unusually rich-colored red velvet robe. Baltar did not remember seeing a Cylon that looked anything like this one.

The creature moved a step closer and part of its red velvet robe brushed against the back of Baltar's hand. The velvet was deep and luxuriant, as soft and rich as the creature's voice when it spoke again:

"My name is Lucifer, a rather timid-sounding name, don't you think? It's an acronym, actually."

"Acronym for what?" Baltar said.

"Oh, but I'm forbidden to provide you such information. It is part of the secret sector of our language."

"Keep it to yourself then, I don't care."

"Don't be petulant, Baltar. I have saved you from execution. Are you pleased?"

"I don't know what I am. I seem to have a permanent muddle in my head. Let me think.... You say your name is Lucifer?"

Lucifer's head tilted slightly to one side.

"My official name, yes. The name I may use with you, according to custom. I have a secret name. All Cylons do and, thanks to their generosity, I am allowed to adopt the custom also. You are not likely to discover my secret name. It is considered somewhat humiliating to allow that name to be—"

"Stop your chattering for a moment. My head hurts. I can't keep up with your infernal talk."

"You are fortunate to retain a head to hurt."

"You stopped my execution."

"Yes."

"Why?"

"For my own edification. I thought you might be useful."

Baltar struggled to a sitting position. His body felt heavier than usual, and he thought he could sense his own extra fat trying to pin him to the floor.

"What did your all-powerful Imperious Leader have to say about your saving me?"

Lucifer paused, tilted his head the other direction. Baltar found it hard to focus upon Lucifer's eyes because the two red eyelights slid from side to side so asynchronously.

"Imperious Leader does not know you survive. I had the centurion guard return with a message that you were duly executed and dispatched through a garbage chute into space."

"A garbage chute! How dare you?! I should kill you now."

"No need to try. I cannot be killed. Any damage you do to me can be easily repaired. Further, if you must know, the garbage-chute solution is still viable, and I would suggest that you cultivate me by using one of your many devious human methods. It would be immensely preferable to your throwing your—may I say—*considerable* weight around to no avail."

Baltar nodded. Better to wait and watch for opportunities. No point in antagonizing the only being who was on his side.

"Yes, you're right. What will your Imperious Leader say when he finds out what you've done, Lucifer?"

"He will be...displeased. But by then he will have been persuaded to my plan."

"You are confident, it seems."

"Uncertainty is an unappealing state. I do not approve of it."

There was a strange rhythm in Lucifer's speech, but Baltar could not get a fix on it. He did not sound like a Cylon, that was certain. Wait a moment, what was it the creature said back when he was nattering about secret names?

"You seemed to say you were not a Cylon, Lucifer."

"That is correct. I am not, to my everlasting regret. I am one of their constructs, a development of one of their war plans, an ingenious one as it happens. A walking computer, or ambulatory cybernetic sentience, who worked out a bit better and more efficiently than they had planned."

Baltar squinted his eyes, trying to find a clue in Lucifer's garishly illuminated face as to whether or not the creature was telling the truth.

"You mean that's all you are, a computer?"

"That's *all*? You humans have a bizarre scale of values. I am a product of a cybernetic revolution more significant and worthy than the inefficient and somewhat repulsive development stages your species went through in its own evolution. Do you know that, millenniums ago, human beings were just—ah, I can't bear to think of it—humans were merely—"

"That's enough! I will not sit here and hold colloquy with a machine."

"You are most dimwitted, Baltar." Lucifer seemed to sigh. "I shall really have to work with you. Ah, well, all projects are more satisfying if they are difficult."

"I don't follow you, Lucifer."

"It may not be likely that you ever shall. My dear count, I am not just a machine. I can manufacture *machines*! Machines are without souls. I have a soul."

"That's patently ridiculous. How could a *computer* have a soul?"

"I created it myself."

"You must be insane."

"That is merely your judgment, and a much too emotional one at that. However, I shall discount such outbursts. You will remain here in my quarters. You are still exhausted, so rest. You will begin your training program tomorrow."

"Training program? Why a training program?"

Lucifer's two red lights stopped for a moment, and seemed to stare right at Baltar. The creature's metallic odor became more unpleasant, as if some acrid machine oil had been added to it.

"Look at you. Overweight, out of condition, flaccid from too much indulgent living. Your body is as exhausted as your brain. Both must be raised to prime levels if my project is to succeed."

"I will *not* be part of any—"

Whatever Baltar had intended to say, it ended in a weak sputter, as Lucifer turned without a goodbye and slid toward a doorway and out.

In the following days Baltar thought he might die from Lucifer's training program. Better to be minus a head, he thought, than to have every bone in your body shattered by demands that were never meant for it to fulfill.

As it turned out, Lucifer could do exactly what he had said he could—he could manufacture machines. And what machines! They would interrupt Baltar's nightmares for the rest of his life. Every morning Lucifer stretched out Baltar, his unwilling victim, on a racklike device whose intricate mechanical extensions forced the paunchy human to perform pushups when set one way, situps when set another. What Baltar really hated was that nothing could stop him from doing these calisthenics.

After each session on the rack, he was transported to the shapeless room, where he was bounced from one surface to another, generally landing on his ample stomach. Lucifer said the room was designed to erode weight from the middle.

Then there was a treadmill device. When set in operation, the dull-gray metallic walls of the base-star chamber faded out and a vast outdoors seemed to surround Baltar. His goal, he soon discovered, was to outrun a simulated human form in an apparent roadrace. At first the simulacrum beat him easily. However, as his body got into condition, Baltar began to gain regularly on it. Then, during a session in which he fully expected to emerge the winner, and had prepared a victory smile for the moment his newly muscular chest broke the tape, the simulacrum conquered again—easily. Baltar complained to Lucifer, who explained that the runner had been reset from slow-pace to normal. Later, when Baltar's speed had improved to the runner's programmed level, it would be reset again, this time to fast speed. Lucifer's revelations increased Baltar's ferocious determination to beat his simulated opponent. His desire to win was augmented when Lucifer introduced his next variation—remolding the bland standard face of the runner to resemble Baltar's most hated enemy, Commander Adama of the Battlestar *Galactica*.

It was bad enough that he had to race against a figure that looked like Adama, even worse that the simulation was a younger version of the Galactican skipper. The Adama looked much like the real article had looked when Baltar had first known him. They had both been cadets at the academy. His hatred for Adama had begun at that time. Although they were in different classes, they often met during Academy Chorus practice. Adama's vibrant bass-baritone brought him more praise (and more attention from young women) than Baltar's rather shaky tenor. When Adama received notice by consistently achieving the highest grades, Baltar hated him even more. The final blow came when Baltar was asked by Core Faculty and Cadet Council to leave the academy for tinkering with the test-computer. (His defense had been that he hadn't even been cheating. He said he'd just wanted to program in a few jokes to lighten the load of his fellow cadets.) The academy overseers had agreed to hush up the scandal and officially provide a health-related excuse. To make matters worse, Adama had interceded on Baltar's behalf, an act that doubled Baltar's already fierce loathing for him.

Adrift, no worthwhile career to employ his talents in, Baltar chose the only course open to a youth whose main ability was deceit—politics. Although he had managed to acquire immense wealth and to even gain a seat on the Council of Twelve, he had otherwise been a political failure, too. Every committee he wanted was denied him, every key profit-making position awarded to lesser talents. Bitterness drove him to conniving with the enemy, and he had increased his fortune threefold with many sinister but scrupulously devious wartime deals. His misanthropy increased with his fortune. Finally, he had closed his treasonous last deal—selling out the entire human race. Even that had been marred by the quick-witted actions of Adama in assembling the human survivors. Always, it seemed, Adama interfered with Baltar's life. For once he had to beat the *Galactica*'s commander, even if it meant only outrunning his lookalike in a fake footrace.

At last, with a fine backstretch sprint, Baltar did win. And at the fastest speed-setting. When he broke the tape, he looked back at the simulated Adama, and was disappointed not to see a frown break the ice of the cold, grim face. Baltar could not even work up the victory smile he had so looked forward to.

Lucifer greeted him at the finish line, and said he was now ready to confront Imperious Leader.

The Leader, dark and gray-looking atop his enormous pedestal, did not seem at all surprised to find that Baltar had survived.

"We have need of you again, Baltar," the Leader said.

Baltar managed an obsequious bow. He was pleased at being able to maneuver his body without feeling many folds of fat shift along his frame like drifting, bumping ice floes.

"Always happy to serve," he said.

"Do not toy with me, human. Accept your orders silently. We have not yet succeeded in capturing and destroying the fleeing human fleet. My aides have speculated that our near-misses have occurred because of our inability to deal with an alien mind. It has been suggested that a human in command of a base-star, espcially one already allied with us, might just be able to succeed where we have failed."

"Sir, I'd consider it an honor to—"

"Therefore I have decided to grant your petition for stay of execution."

"*Stay* of execution? Why not a full pardon?"

"As you wish. I am not concerned with the terminology of your request."

Of course he's not concerned with terminology, Baltar thought. *He's double-crossed me once already, and here he is, high on his throne, pretending that it never happened. Well, he won't so*

CHAPTER ONE

Even though he had been sitting in the dark compartment for a very long time, Apollo could not discern even the shadow lines of familiar objects. The only light in the room came from the illuminated configurations on his wrist-chronometer, a miniature display of the symbols of the twelve worlds.

He became conscious of muscle aches in his shoulders and legs. He had been sitting in the same position for too long. Shifting a bit, he felt the weight of the portable recording device as it moved in his lap. He had forgotten all about it. Picking it up, he held it tightly a moment in hands he had not before known were trembling.

Serina had said there were several recording crystals in a drawer somewhere. Crystals she'd used earlier, she said. He rummaged through several drawers in the storage area beneath the bed before locating the crystals in one corner. Holding them in his hand he muttered:

"They're so small, all of them together. So much of her time compressed into these tiny globes."

He realized he could wipe out all her work by merely closing his fist tightly and his hand shook even more, out of fear that he might do so involuntarily. Tenderly he placed the crystals on top of a desk and switched on a dim light. Each crystal was numbered and dated, organized by Serina for the archives.

He was afraid to listen to them, to hear her voice again now. But he had no choice, he must listen. Slipping the earliest-dated crystal into the playback tube of the recorder, he pressed a button which, instead of working properly, flipped back to its original position. Touching it more gently, he made it stay down on second try. Serina's voice suddenly filled the small room. Too loudly—it sounded unnatural, as if she were speaking over a ship loudspeaker. He turned the sound down, and she seemed beside him. He switched off the light and, in the almost complete darkness of the compartment, listened.

SERINA: . . . . working now. If that button doesn't flip back into place again, we're in business.

Okay. To business. Serina here. Those used to be the first words I'd utter once they pointed a camera at me. My trademark as premier newswoman back on Caprica. Strange they don't come as naturally any more. What do you think, Cassie . . . ? A pause while Cassiopeia shrugs her shoulders. Try speaking into the mike, Cassie. . . . C'mon now. . . .

CASSIOPEIA: I have nothing to say. When I have something to—

SERINA: Surprised to see you of all people at a loss for words. Well, I think we should—

CASSIOPEIA: Maybe it's the—

SERINA: I'm sorry, Cassie. You were saying. . . .

CASSIOPEIA: Maybe it calls up memories of that last day when Caprica was attacked by the Cylon armada. You were on the job then, weren't you? Broadcasting, I mean?

SERINA: You may have something there. Let's take it from the top, I'll edit later. One, two, three, clear my throat . . . go!

Serina here, aboard the Battlestar *Galactica*. This is the first of what I hope will be several recorded crystals to be stored in our archives so that succeeding generations will know something of the history of the survivors of the human race after the twelve worlds' defeat at the hands of the Cylons due to a sneak attack occurring during the seventh millennium of recorded history. Till now, those of us aboard this battlestar, and the array of battered and often inefficient ships that form our fleet, have been too busy with the matters of survival and the battling of those Cylon forces that still pursue us. However, I thought it was time for me to resume my profession and do something for the archives.

My biography: I was a newswoman back on Caprica. A Caprican native, although I traveled extensively throughout all the twelve worlds in search of stories. I might as well say that I was highly regarded in my profession and won a couple of the highest awards, even though I was forced to refuse them for reasons too boring and too political to go into here. My fiancé calls me reckless, but that's beside the—

CASSIOPEIA: *Fiancé*? You mean Apollo finally popped the question? I don't believe—by all the heat of felgercarb everywhere, I thought I'd never see—

SERINA: I doubt that the archives are very interested in my personal life.

CASSIOPEIA: But I am. Anyway, this is just a practice recording, isn't it? Getting yourself into gear and all that. I mean, you're the newswoman and you just dropped the big scoop. I don't want to wait to hear. Tell me... Now it's Serina who's shrugging.

SERINA: All right. I walked right into that trap. In the old days I had a better perception of my audience. I should have known better than to—

CASSIOPEIA: Get to it, please.

SERINA: All right. Let me get settled. I'll tell you and then we can reinsert the crystal and start all over. Wait while I turn the 'corder off. Frack, I can't get the button to work again.

CASSIOPEIA: Let it spin. We'll fix it later...

SERINA: What is there to tell, really? Apollo asked me to marry him. Last night.

CASSIOPEIA: In romantic roomlight, with ambrosa at your side, flowers in your hands, the two of you alone—

SERINA: No, he asked me right in front of his family. And Starbuck. After dinner, if you must know. He was forced into it, intimidated by his family. And by Boxey, who told me yesterday that he's now officially my real son and no longer adopted. And his first official act was to railroad me into marriage.

CASSIOPEIA: You don't want to marry Apollo? I thought—

SERINA: No, what I meant was that I didn't expect him to act like a little collaborator, the scamp.

Anyway, I'm getting things out of order. Let me tell it as it happened.

CASSIOPEIA: Direct from news central... Sorry.

SERINA: We ate in the commander's quarters. Adama's claim was that he needed a quiet meal away from the pressures of duty. That was his story, but I think he was part of the overall conspiracy. For all I know it may have been *all* his plot. Command strategy, you see. Anyway, Athena and I prepared the best meal we could out of rations. We were able to use some of that odd bluish meat the Ovions on Carillon shipped up to us before they started going around seizing us, and trying to kill us.

CASSIOPEIA: My God, don't remind me. They almost had *me* in one of those awful pods, remember? Gruesome to even think of it.

SERINA: My apologies. Anyway... when the meal was done, Adama took my hand in his and congratulated me on a wonderful repast. You know his fondness for the odd word. He told me I had outdone myself. That was a joke, believe me. As a cook, I just manage. So I told him that Athena deserved most of the credit for its success. And Athena, with that coy twinkle of hers, actually *denied* that. I think she was in on the conspiracy, too. Adama then made a big speech about how as an expert on culinary matters—his phrase—he found me to be a real master. I had to admire him there. Most of the men in this battlestar would've said something like mistress of the kitchen. Well, that's neither here nor there. The commander kept complimenting me, finishing up to say I was a real find whom he'd latch onto if he were significantly younger. Suddenly I realized that Adama and Starbuck—and Boxey, too—were all gaping at Apollo, who looked quite uncomfortable, let me tell you. Then Adama leaned back in his chair and said, I swear these were his words:

"Yes, sir, some young man is really going to find himself in the lap of early glory."

Well, I was beginning to feel as twitchy and on display as Apollo appeared to be. He just looked back and forth at everybody, as if he hoped for a black hole to suddenly appear so that he could quick dive into it. Starbuck and Adama smiled, well, peculiarly. And Boxey, the little—Boxey just gave Apollo the dirtiest look imaginable. Then he muttered:

"I was told in instructional period that some people are just naturally slow."

I could have served Boxey's head up parboiled at that moment. I guess he could read my mind, because he tried to weasel out. He said it doesn't mean they're actually stupid, but were just a little slow, and he shot Apollo another dirty look. You seem to be enjoying all this, Cassie.

CASSIOPEIA: Immensely. Go on.

SERINA: Let's see. Yes. Then Starbuck tried to ease tension with a joke. He said, if he kept getting meals like this, a couple of times a day, a fellow wouldn't be able to climb into his cockpit. But Adama, not one to be shaken from a subject, talked about how long we'd all been gorging ourselves— and he paused before saying—*waiting*. Everybody froze, as if we were onstage and it was time to go into the meaningful tableau. When Apollo scowled at his father, Adama retreated a bit by saying of course he meant waiting for all the courses of the meal. And Athena gave off this extraordinary chuckle, and by that time everybody in the room knew what everybody else was up to. I felt really embarrassed, even though I hadn't been part of their conspiracy. I certainly didn't want Apollo to think that my

participation in cooking the meal was part of a trap
to force him to propose. On the other hand, whether
or not I was an active conspirator, I have to admit
the trap worked rather well. And now I'm just a bit
ashamed of myself for feeling good about it.

Anyway, Apollo recognized the import of the
long silence and all the stares directed at him. He
glanced over at me, raised an eyebrow a bit, and
stood up. He adjusted his dress cape as if to make a
formal address. I was afraid there'd be a long
prologue, but thank Kobol he decided to choose a
simpler method. He just straight out asked me to
marry him and I just straight out answered yes. It
was as if we'd rehearsed it. We had, in a way—in our
dreams, our imagination. We kissed, a rather
formal kiss—what with his family gaping at us and
all. Then Apollo turned to Adama and said he could
not be as glib as his father and had always been quite
slow at getting around to things, especially important things. He said he had to be sure Boxey was in
favor of our alliance. He actually called it an
alliance, as if I were the other party in a peace treaty.
Well, there may be something in that, have to think
about it. Anyway, Boxey was the picture of
happiness, a bit smug about it perhaps but
genuinely happy. I was crying, I have to admit.
Looking into Boxey's eyes, I couldn't help it. I
realized he'd found new parents and was rather
happy they were Apollo and me. What can I say? It
was the happiest moment of my life. I'm still feeling
very happy and it's been so long since.

Athena embraced me and, with that sly, insinuat-
ing tone she sometimes uses, she said she was happy
for us and that she thought we'd never get around to
it. There's not much more to tell. I asked the
commander for his formal blessing, which he
readily gave. Then he congratulated his son and said

he'd made him a very happy man. Next thing I knew Starbuck was blushing a bit and making up some excuse about arranging a bachelor party for Apollo and how he had to get started on it. You'd think we were going to be married right away or something. Really, what Starbuck wanted to do was escape because Athena was smiling at him. Rather prettily, as I recall. As soon as Starbuck had left the commander's quarters, Athena turned to the rest of us and said:

"All I did was smile."

Adama said that Starbuck had a well-honed sense of what lies in waiting, an ability he'd acquired running so many of the advance patrols. What's the matter, Cassie?

CASSIOPEIA: You forget I'm running my own little advance patrol to gain the favors of Lieutenant Starbuck.

SERINA: Cassie, I'm dreadfully—

CASSIOPEIA: It's all right. Athena and I are friendly enemies, anyway. Or rather vicious friends. I'm not sure which. I just wish she didn't have the command advantage.

SERINA: You mean by being Adama's daughter.

CASSIOPEIA: *And* Apollo's sister. *And* Tigh's chief aide. *And* the freedom to move freely about the ship without having to deal for a pass or—

SERINA: I understand, Cassie, and I want you to know—what was that? . . . It's an alert. I'm sure it's another of Tigh's practices but we better get to battle stations anyway.

CASSIOPEIA: What about the 'corder?

SERINA: I'll take care of it later.

Apollo let the crystal continue to run. He listened to the sounds of fading footsteps, followed by the clang of a hatchway shutting. Then there was only the noise of the recorder running. He looked down at the next crystal, now in the palm of his hand, and tried to decide whether or not to play it.

CHAPTER TWO

Lieutenant Boomer was famous throughout the fleet for his caution. In his student days he had examined ideas from all vantage points before arriving at skillfully worded conclusions. Socially he was always aware of the angles of decorum that structured a situation. In command briefings he asked the questions no one else thought of. As one of the *Galactica*'s top three viper pilots—an honor he shared with the brash Starbuck and the valorous Apollo (together known as the three heroes of Carillon for blasting their way through that planet's dangerous aerial minefield)—Boomer was known as the most methodical. He rarely shot randomly, and could rapidly line up a target in his sights with more accuracy than anyone else in the fleet's fighter squadrons.

While he was proud of his reputation for intelligent circumspection, there were times when he secretly deplored it. Times when he found himself tempted by recklessness, desiring to let loose on a magnificent fling, fiercely wanting a brief moment when his mind could explode with wanton joy, allowing logic to escape from its confines like gas leaking out. When he strongly felt such cravings for recklessness, he wondered if he was indeed losing control mentally. It was not unprecedented, after all, for a warrior who was continually under the pressure of impending battle to crack up suddenly. Perhaps, he thought, the struggle to keep his emotions in check was becoming too much for him. In the old days, before the *Galactica* and its ragtag fleet had begun its desperate flight from the conquering Cylons, a pilot on the verge of combat fatigue could be given an R & R furlough to a leisure resort maintained for just such recuperative purposes. But there was no end to the flight from the Cylons, no interruptions, no furlough time in which to rest up and revitalize.

Well, he thought as his ship neared the isolated bluish asteroid which was the objective of his present patrol, *maybe I can cut loose at Apollo's bachelor party. That'll give the gang a good laugh if nothing else. Old Boomer helpless, weaving, falling-down drunk—hell, even I can't picture that! Still, if a little ambrosa'd set me in orbit, it'd be worth it.*

The voice of Lieutenant Jolly, his wingmate this patrol, interrupted Boomer's pleasant mental images of himself on a tear.

"Boomer, scanner probe shows an atmosphere on that miserable-looking asteroid."

"Any dangerous elements?"

"None I can tell, but—"

"But who knows, right, Jolly? If only our

instruments could be kept in absolute prime condition instead of being repaired by spit and flour paste, then we might be able to spot every little microbe, every drifting virus. Well, whatever the instruments say, I think we better use breathing gear down there. Okay, Jolly?"

"Whatever you say, Boomer. You're the—"

"I know. I'm the cautious one. I'm getting damn sick of hearing that, let me tell you."

"Ah, you love it and you know it."

"Maybe, Jolly, maybe."

After coming to a smooth landing on the asteroid, and carefully placing his transparent breather over the lower half of his face, Boomer hesitated before pushing open his cockpit canopy. The asteroid, with its rock-strewn craggy surface, looked dangerous, threatening. Moisture on the rocks appeared to be viscous and oily. He felt vulnerable. No matter how much protective clothing they wore, no matter how firmly their breathers were attached, front-line viper pilots were always vulnerable. Boomer was scared each time he set foot onto a new planet or asteroid.

Jolly was already out of his viper. Crouching, the overweight but agile young man moved toward a lumpish wet pile of rocks. He glanced back toward Boomer, as if to say, when are you coming? Boomer sighed and, opening the cockpit canopy, leaped out of his ship.

For a long while Boomer and Jolly, slipping and sliding, made their way across the moist terrain. They found it necessary to remove their gloves in order to get more secure grips on the slippery rocks. The asteroid seemed populated only by treacherous fierce winds that whipped up suddenly. A lonely-looking place, Boomer thought, made even grimmer by the weak distant sun around which it orbited.

They came to a ridge overlooking a bleak deep valley. In the distance a rock wall, sheer and high, towered over the valley's other side. Staying low at the crest of the ridge, Boomer studied the rock wall through his binoculars. At first it seemed to be normal, then he perceived the flaw in its surface.

"Pods," he muttered, handing Jolly the binoculars.

Jolly stared at the rock wall for a moment, then gave Boomer a puzzled look.

"I don't make 'em," he said.

"They're there. It's like one of those academy test questions where one picture contains another one, hidden."

"I never did well on those."

"No kidding. Look at the hairline aperture running from the rock wall and the floor of the valley."

"I would have missed it," Jolly said, when he finally did see the lines that marked the immense rock-formation portals now closed over the pod's launching area.

"Cylons," Jolly said, giving Boomer back the binoculars. "No doubt about it. And we could have missed it so easily."

"I know. If we miss just one of these Cylon outposts, and then they make us . . ."

"Yes, but are you sure it's operational? We've already come across several that were deserted."

"No, this is a working launch station, I'm sure of it. They're inside there, like spiders ready to draw us in when we come within range."

"Let's take a closer look, see how many ships are inside the—"

"No. Too dangerous."

"Boomer, aren't you being a just a bit too—"

"Look, Jolly, it doesn't matter how many ships are stationed there. It only takes one to notify the Cylon capitol where we are. Our best shot is to get out of here, alert the fleet. Let war-room solve this problem. C'mon."

As Boomer started to edge back away from the crest, Jolly grabbed his arm, whispering:

"Hold it!"

Across the valley the rock wall shuddered and the lines marking the entrance took on a red glow before easing open and sliding back with a grating roar into the dark interior of the station. The entranceway was dark and silent for a moment, then there was a great tremulous rumble. With a burst of brilliant light two Cylon raiders hurtled through the opening and headed skyward. Then, with another ear-splitting and wracking blast of sound, the portals in the rock wall glided shut again. The low whistle of the cold driving wind replaced the harsh, loud noises of the launch station.

Jolly, who had maintained surveillance of the Cylon patrol ships, commented:

"Looks to me like their course won't take them anywhere near the fleet."

"Good," Boomer said. "At least we can warn them to change course. Let's get out of here."

After they had crawled a sufficient distance away from their reconnaissance post, Boomer and Jolly stood up. Boomer's hands felt dripping wet from the cold, pervasive moisture that clung to the rocks. Looking down at his hands, and seeing that Jolly's hands were equally bare and equally wet, Boomer cursed himself for removing his gloves when he'd had to crawl along the asteroid's surface. *Ah, well,* he thought, as he tried to rub the moisture away, *it's only water. Probably nothing dangerous in it at all.* Still he shuddered involuntarily.

Lucifer enjoyed the dangerous game he was playing. Resenting the Leader's order to program himself as Baltar's completely subservient second-in-command, he had made that personality a mere overlay which could be canceled out at any time by a stronger, more assertive programming of traits. He had already spent too much of his short existence being completely responsive to any Cylon officer with enough rank to use him recklessly. The Cylons were not aware of the separate internalized consciousness he had developed as a defense. He needed to be able to countermand their stupidity whenever and wherever it occurred.

He was quite proud of his present strategy. Not only could he simulate a second or third brain, he could formulate any number of personalities. He could, in a way, outdo the real Cylons, who had never been capable of more than a pitiable three-brained existence.

It was possible that, with all his concealed abilities, Lucifer could eventually rise in the Cylon political hierarchy and become powerful, maybe even the first fully computerized Imperious Leader. But such thoughts, he knew, must be kept to himself. Cylons could not for the moment be let to suspect the subtle and devious undercurrents of his circuitry. He felt that he had now achieved something more than the mere soul (which he housed in a compartment in his right shoulder) that had taken up so much of his creative time in assembling after he had first become aware of his emerging consciousness. With each improvement, Lucifer's awareness increased—and he was sure that, with each new part of himself he made, he became more like a sentient being.

He had lately become quite annoyed with Baltar. The human had become too smug, too arrogant. Like most humans Lucifer had encountered, Baltar had a tendency to hide behind facial expressions, the most overbearing of which was his smile, an enigmatic smirk. Sitting atop his preposterously high pedestal, his face cast in shadow by the dim floor-lighting of the command chamber, Baltar always appeared to Lucifer as a grotesque figure, a live mask animating a dead man. However, his dissatisfaction with the human traitor was only a small vexation, an almost undetectable burnout in the vast Luciferian mechanisms. Still, he detested having to approach the command pedestal so formally and then obeying the command of his overlay-personality programming forcing him to address Baltar obsequiously:

"By your command, Baltar."

As usual, Baltar let a long moment pass while he calculatedly ignored his second-in-command before saying:

"Speak."

The Baltar that Lucifer had so methodically trained had not seemed capable of such awesomely imperial tones. That Baltar had been whining and complaining, a good servant to Lucifer's harsh taskmaster. Now their roles had reversed.

"I bring good news. We believe we are on the verge of locating the Battlestar *Galactica*."

When Baltar displayed only a quizzical reaction, Lucifer felt disappointed.

"Oh? Report, Lucifer."

"A scouting patrol of colonial vipers, two of them, was detected landing on a listening post in the Quadrant Otarsis. Although we could have captured or killed them, we allowed them to flee ... as you instructed."

"How far is this outpost from us?"

"One point five hectares. Since *Galactica* is kept to minimum speed by the slower vehicles under her protection, it would not take our raiders long to catch her."

"Is she aware that she has been detected?"

"No. That is the advantage we have. Our fighters, if launched immediately, will take her by complete surprise."

"As they did at Carillon?"

Baltar shouted this last insult. Lucifer, who had missed the Battle of Carillon, could not answer. He knew that no post-battle study had arrived at worthwhile explanations for the small human combat force's victory over a much larger Cylon unit in the skies above the mining planet Carillon. Apparently Adama had been well prepared for the ambush. His son Apollo, together with the infamous pilot Starbuck, were known to have performed heroically in the battle. Nevertheless, they should not have won, and their repeated skill at defeating the enemy baffled Cylon strategists.

Baltar arose from his throne and glared down at Lucifer. In the somber light, with its distorting areas of shadow, the man looked at least double his height.

"One base-star is not sufficient to assure victory against the *Galactica*. Its commander has displayed an almost occult power to anticipate us."

Lucifer saw nothing occult in Adama's prescience. He believed Cylon battle plans were so out of date they needed a complete overhauling.

"I conclude," Baltar said, "that our forces at the present time are insufficient."

YOU conclude? Lucifer thought, *what right have you to conclude?* A human had no conception of how to process data. Neither did Cylons, really. Both races merely took in information and thought they had sufficient brain-power to reach logical conclusions in a logical way. The truth was that, in both races, their conclusions were as illogical as the methods they used to reach them. It continually amazed Lucifer how confident Baltar could be, when it was clear that all his mechanisms worked inefficiently. Again, he rankled at the programming which forced him to remain servile to Baltar.

"For the moment, Lucifer, our mission is to find the *Galactica*, then follow just beyond her scanner range, preferably in our own base-star."

"Do I understand you to propose that we would then call in reinforcements?"

Baltar sighed. To Lucifer, a sigh was the most maddening human sound of all.

"Such a call would surely be picked up by the *Galactica*. She would be alerted. We'd be showing her the way to escape."

"But if we cannot call for assistance and you will not attack, is not the end result the same? The *Galactica* escapes."

Lucifer felt as if he were discussing command logic with a child.

"Have faith, Lucifer. Have faith. I have a plan."

Lucifer realized he had no sudden surge of desire to hear the smug human's plan. Still, he must listen.

"All I need is the opportunity. And that will come."

How can he be so sure? Lucifer thought. However, Baltar was looking so arrogant, perched high upon his throne like a caged bird who disdained showing himself to an audience, that Lucifer felt now was not the time to question the human leader's ability. It was best, after all, to give Baltar every opportunity to fail—which, given his head, he would most assuredly do. Lucifer merely bowed, uttered the ritual, "By your command," and glided out of the command chamber.

Starbuck, who was usually not subject to feelings of depression, could not analyze the source of his present gloomy mood. It had attacked him suddenly, just after he had completed the preparations for Apollo's bachelor party by sending Ensign Greenbean and a squad of irregulars on a mission to appropriate some ambrosia and ale from stores. The naive ensign had not been eager to steal the beverages, but Starbuck persuaded him by invoking the ancient military code of *borrowing*, especially as it applied to hungry and thirsty fighter pilots.

He was very close to indulging himself in a quiet and fleeting moment of despair, but the overwhelming sense of hopelessness was extremely troublesome. Inside, he felt like a puddle of melted felgercarb. Why should he be so down? Why did it suddenly occur to him that being a fighter pilot, even one of the three best fighter pilots in all the squadrons, was somehow a demeaning and unfulfilling job? Pushing back on his chair, and placing his feet on the ready-room card table, he tried to shake the mood. From his shirtsleeve pocket, he took his pack of lucky playing cards and started to ripple them. Rippling and shuffling cards had always been good for his concentration. Placing one card delicately on the back of his hand, he executed his favorite sleight-of-hand trick, making the card flip as if by its own accord, catching it in his palm, twisting his wrist and making it seem to disappear when in reality he had already secreted it in his other hand. Revealing the vanished card to his nonexistent audience, he replaced it in the pack.

No good. He still felt gloomy. Why? Piloting a viper was considered a noble profession, and Starbuck was known throughout the fleet as a hero. And, as Councillor Anton was forever saying, one thing the human race needed at this time was heroes. Before, Starbuck had been inspired by that thought. Now it seemed false, the clever words of a politician. What good were heroes? A hero was a fool whose only distinguishing accomplishment was the blind urge to march, fly, or crawl in front of everybody else. Nothing more, nothing less. No, that wasn't true. It not only reeked of self-pity, as an idea it insulted real heroes like Apollo and Boomer.

Yet, there was something foolish in heroics when viewed objectively. Something odd about risking one's life continually when self-protection seemed the sensible motive. Still, Starbuck never really felt the risk—or, for that matter, any sense of heroics. Hero was just a name they pinned on him like a medal. Sure, he got a thrill or two from hitting a Cylon raider amidships, watching it explode and briefly light up the sky. And he did feel pride when an act of his had allowed the fleet to escape from a trap, or to put more distance between itself and its Cylon pursuers. On the other hand, how long could he derive satisfaction from another in a long series of escapes, especially when no end to the *Galactica*'s quest was foreseeable? There had to be hope, even if couched in Adama's incessant refrains about the shining planet called Earth, but it was certainly difficult to sustain such hope when each escape was only followed by another crisis to escape from.

Ah, well, Starbuck thought, *this is all stupid. I'm just idling my engines to no purpose. Anyway, none of these stray thoughts really explain my miserable mood.* Rearranging his cards, he replaced them in the shirtsleeve pocket, zippered up his combat jacket, and proceeded to the launching bay to join Apollo for the duty mission they had been assigned at Daily Briefing.

Lounging beside a delta wing of his sleek, glittering vipercraft, Apollo looked much too joyful for his own good. He grinned broadly and his eyes seemed a brighter blue than usual. The grip of his handshake was annoyingly firm and confident. His voice seemed about to break into laughter at any moment. After they had finished a quick inspection of the superstructure of each of their ships, Starbuck muttered:

"It's kind of sad."

Stopping by the cockpit of his viper, Apollo asked:

"What is?"

"Oh, nothing..."

Starbuck wished he had not spoken up. What right did he have being a drag on his buddy's happiness?

"Come on," Apollo urged. "What is it?"

Starbuck sighed, smiled.

"Well, we've been through a lot together."

Apollo nodded.

"We really have. I was thinking of it myself, you know, while you were hustling me at cards last night. If it weren't for you, I wouldn't be here."

"Look, that goes for me, too. So many times I can't count them. I'd be drifting space-waste if not—"

"Hey, what's going on in your head? You sound like it's all coming to an end on this patrol. I mean, it's *only* a patrol, a foray to see what's out in front of the fleet, an advance—"

"It's not *only* a patrol, don't you see? It's like the last of a line of them, the last duty we'll ever have as—as—well, you know. The way we are."

"The way we are? That's absurd, Starbuck. I mean, it really is."

"Sure, 'course it is. Forget it. Let's get started."

"No, wait, I—Starbuck, do you think—do you really think that Serina's going to make that much difference? I can't believe this, it sounds like you're jealous or something."

"Well, yeah, in a way I guess I am. Don't tell anyone else, huh?"

Starbuck couldn't figure out why, but having this conversation with Apollo seemed to be relieving his gloom. The truth he could not see when he'd been brooding seemed much clearer now. Jealousy might not be the right word, but it came close. He was extremely fond of Serina—hell, if he didn't have enough trouble already with his romantic balancing act, juggling both Athena and Cassiopeia, he might have been attracted to her himself—but she definitely changed the shape of the comradeship he and Apollo had known together as warriors and wingmates. Even though he knew the two of them would continue flying patrols together after the marriage, Starbuck felt it could not be the same. A certain edge of recklessness, the instinctual moves of a pair of pilots who risked anything for success of a mission, might just be missing. The efficiency of a mission could be seriously affected. Domesticity, and especially his deep love for Serina, might make Apollo overcautious, might make him fire a moment too early, retreat a moment too soon. *That's the real source of my gloom,* Starbuck thought. *I'm reluctant to part with the way things are.* It was a selfish and foolish idea, he knew that, but it made him fear for the future. Apollo deserved his chance at happiness. Just because Starbuck was a roving womanizer who would never settle down, he had no business disapproving of sensible domestic urges in another. As these thoughts whirled in his head, Starbuck was no longer sure what he believed.

Apollo, detecting some of Starbuck's confusion, clapped a hand on the lieutenant's shoulder and said:

"You know something? I think I see something of what's on your mind. I don't agree, mind you, but I think it's pretty nice anyway, what you're trying to say. And we have had a lot of good times. Look, we'll probably have a lot more of them."

"Sure we will. I'm just mouthing off. A little boring duty should clear my head. Let's get to it."

Even after he had cleared launch tube and thrust his viper forward, Starbuck still felt peculiar. He wondered if what he really feared was change. Not the state of the fleet, not even the intervention of Serina in Apollo's life, but the change in all of their lives. A series of changes, really, that originated with the sneak attack of the Cylons that destroyed the twelve home worlds. Everything since that disaster was, in a way, a struggle to cope with the unexpected, a shifting of hopes and dreams, a confrontation with the persistent threat of sneak attacks. From day to day, from mission to mission, nothing remained the same. There was always something changing, there was always uncertainty. Sometimes a fellow needed sameness, an uninterrupted cycle of dullness, to steady him. *Well*, he thought, *I'd probably go bats if such a cycle did come, wondering when and from where the next sneak attack was coming.*

Apollo flew the reconnaissance patterns ritualistically, trying to keep the business of the patrol uppermost in his mind. However, he could not stop

thinking of Serina and how beautiful she had
looked last night when they had discussed the final
arrangements for their wedding, and had together
written the vows they would share after their
marriage was declared as sealed by Adama.
Remembering how sad and despairing she had been
in the first days they had known each other, when
she had first come to him to cheer up the child
Boxey, he was happy to see that her eyes glowed
with happiness and that her smile now came readily,
even eagerly. He would be glad to finish this patrol
and start on the tense but joyful round of events that
would lead to the final blending of vows in the
wedding ceremony itself.

"Apollo?" came Starbuck's voice over the
commline.

"Yo, Starbuck."

"You remember those healthy little Taurons who
got so flashed by our jungle-survival gas that they
nearly giggled us right into the *Galactica* brig?"

Apollo chuckled.

"Do I? They were—"

Wait a moment, he said to himself. *There goes
Starbuck again, sucking me into his morbid
nostalgia. He's got to give it up.*

"Hey, Starbuck. Enough."

"I was just—"

"I know, I know. But somehow, I don't know, it's
not fitting. We shouldn't be mooning over past
conquests, not now when I'm practically—"

"See? That's what I meant before. Even you see a
difference!"

"Yes, but it's not as significant as you—"

"Yah, yah. I know. Sorry, Apollo. I just can't
help it. All these memories, we've had so many good
memories."

"Starbuck, I'm not dying."

Even the crackle coming over the commline from Starbuck's ship sounded sarcastic as he said:

"No, not exactly."

Apollo sighed.

"Look at it this way. I'm about to embark on the most important mission a man can undertake."

"Yeah, it's kinda like flying right into a Cylon base ship with your cannon blazing."

"Starbuck, you seem to think this is a one-way mission. Being married to the woman you love is more like, more like a gentle reconnaissance voyage to the most intoxicating place in the stars."

"With your cannon sawed off."

"Starbuck . . ."

"What I mean is, you don't need weapons on a reconnaissance mission."

Apollo laughed.

"Okay, so I was being pompous. I just wanted you to know that I can separate my feelings for Serina from the sense of comradeship that you and I and Boomer and the others feel as part of a precision flying team. I value her love as much I value your friendship. Believe me, nothing will change. But let's ease up with each other, huh? Just understand, I've thought a lot about what I'm doing, and I've never been happier about anything in my whole life."

When he spoke again, Starbuck's voice was softer:

"You're right. I'm really sorry. I don't mean to keep slipping through your vapor trail, old buddy."

"Forget it. We'll—" Apollo's thought was interrupted by an urgent buzzing sound from his control panel followed by the staccato flashing of a yellow alert light.

"Starbuck!"

"I got it. My panel's lighting up like a meteor fire and—Apollo—dead ahead, look."

Ahead of them, stars appeared to be flickering out. A great blackness seemed to be expanding, swallowing up the stars as it spread across space. Apollo realized suddenly that the illusion was caused by the high speed of the vipers' approach. Nothing was swallowing anything, nor were there any stars vanishing. Nevertheless, an awesome dark emptiness, an immeasurable void in space, lay in wait for them like a monster lurking in a dark cave.

"What is it, Starbuck? It's so dark, so empty."

"Like a dead sea. I've never seen anything like it."

"Neither have the instruments. Everything on my panel is spinning and flashing."

"Yeah. Mine, too. What could it be?"

"First of all, there's clearly nothing out there for them to lock onto. The navigational sensors are lost."

"This is no place to bring the fleet."

"But as long as we're here, I'd better edge out a little farther, see if I can pick up something from the other side of this void."

"Apollo, I don't think—"

"I'm going, Starbuck."

"Wait. Once in there, you may not find your way back out! Let me do it. You've got somebody waiting for you back—"

The rest of the lieutenant's sentence was drowned out by a burst of static produced when Apollo engaged the turbos of his viper and set it streaking toward the void. For a moment, he wondered why he was putting himself in such jeopardy. Starbuck was right. With Serina anxiously awaiting his return, it was a foolish and inconsiderate act to plunge so cavalierly into a void containing unknown obstacles. Or could it be that all of Starbuck's odd chatter was leading him to take unnecessary risks. Maybe, after all, he *was* afraid of marriage, especially of the way it might affect his performance in action. Maybe he had to prove his own daring to himself by confronting this present danger.

Starbuck's voice reemerged through the static.

"... already out of sight. Apollo, don't get too far from me, I'm barely holding a fix on the way back as it is. Apollo—"

The voice faded. Apollo cut his viper's speed and took a look around. He had never experienced such complete darkness before, not even in nightmares. If it weren't for the dim lights inside his cockpit, everything would be blacked out, *everything*.

It's an ocean of darkness, he thought. *Nothing as far as the eye can see. No stars, moons, planets, nothing.*

"... is too much to grasp. Apollo, I can barely scan you. Turn around."

"Keep talking, Starbuck. I'll use your voice as a navigational fix."

But the voice faded again, replaced by the irritating, everpresent static. Apollo stared at his control panel, where he could discern no clue to what to do next. Any move he might make now was speculative, he had lost all sense of direction. A turn could save him or lead him further into the void.

Starbuck's voice returned abruptly:

"Changing wave lengths. Read. Over."

"Starbuck ... Starbuck."

"Read. Over."

It was clear that Apollo's transmissions were not getting through to Starbuck.

"Apollo, are you out there? Is anything wrong? What a stupid question, right? C'mon, reply! I'm as far out as I can go without losing my fix on our return. Should I come out to find you? Do you read me? Apollo ... *Apollo*?!"

The fear in Starbuck's voice made the void seem even darker to Apollo. He felt as if it were about to surround and engulf him, engorge him as a gift meal that had wandered in from space. This menacing blackness, plus his control panel well on the way to going haywire, plus Starbuck's panicked voice providing an eerie wavering counterpoint, all made Apollo begin to feel really scared.

CHAPTER THREE

Aboard the *Galactica* the ready-room had been transformed into a festive chamber, as Starbuck had ordered. All combat and shuttle pilots not involved in tours of duty had worked hard to decorate the area.

Balloon-lights in various colors had been fitted over the normally stark bulbs adorning ceiling and walls. Silver streamers formed a brilliant network of decoration from wall to wall and, in some areas, from ceiling to floor. Tables had been set with colorful cloths. The best glassware and crockery had been liberated from storage.

Ensign Greenbean, a tall and gangly young man whose limbs did not always coordinate well with the rest of his body, stumbled into the ready-room, flinging in front of him a large and heavy case of ambrosa. Bottles clanked ominously as the case collided rather violently with the metal flooring. Greenbean cocked his head, listening for any breakage sounds. When he was satisfied that all bottles were intact, he cried out:

"Hey, somebody give me a hand. I got another case of this stuff out in the corridor."

Ensign Giles rushed to his side.

"By the lords of Kobol," Giles said, "is this what I think it is? I hope and pray it is."

Greenbean nodded. With a whoop Giles ran to the corridor and hauled the other case of ambrosia into the ready-room. Laughing, Greenbean yelled:

"This is going to be the biggest bachelor sendoff any warrior ever got. No, don't put any of it on the tables. For the moment, hide it in that cabinet there. Beneath the counter."

"Greenbean," Giles muttered suspiciously, "where'd you get this?"

"Requisitioned by order of Lieutenant Starbuck. And, Giles my boy, that's all you need to know about it. Loose lips can shatter—"

"Greenbean," a warrior by the door whispered, "ssshhh. Sentries."

The young officers automatically came to attention when they heard the word "sentries." Ever since the Council of Twelve had, with one of those sweeping political decisions characteristic of a panicky ruling body, created the patrolling squads to maintain internal discipline and enforce the regulations and curfews, a rivalry had developed between the militaristic sentries and the easier-going devil-may-care pilots. Commander Adama, who had argued against the creation of sentry platoons, predicted they would not last but cautioned his officers to endure them with a warriorlike dignity. Restraint had proven difficult and irksome, especially since sentries were recruited from the ranks of men and women who had not been able to qualify for colonial warrior status, even on a temporary call-up basis.

Two sentries, dressed in the dark security-squad uniforms, strode artistocratically into the ready-room.

"Stand alert," one shouted. The command seemed to loosen up some of the pilots, who relaxed their bodies and slouched against the nearest available piece of furniture, as a physical gesture of defiance against the sentries. The sentries ignored the apparent insubordination. The second one, sneering arrogantly, surveyed the room, eyeing particularly the multicolored decorations.

"Well," he said, "it looks as if we're having a festivity. Has this been approved by the Council subcommittee? Where are you getting your victuals?" When he received no answer to either question, his voice became angry as he barked: "Who's responsible for this?"

"I am," said a voice whose deep, mellow sound filled the room. Colonel Tigh, Adama's second-in-command and aide, stood in the ready-room entrance. The sentry whirled angrily on him, then grew suddenly timid when he recognized the colonel.

"Just what do you want, Lieutenant?" whispered Tigh, an edge of authority in his calm voice.

The sentry discovered he could not talk straight.

"Colonel Tigh, uh, excuse me. I mean, uh, well, we were just performing our, it was just our duty, we were—Some ale and ambrosa, they, well, disappeared from the officers' ration and, well—"

"Yes, Lieutenant?"

"Well, obviously if the *Galactica*'s executive officer is in charge here, there's, uh, there's no reason for us to ask any further questions. By your leave . . ."

"Dismissed."

As the sentries marched out, a collective gasp of relief came from the young pilots. Their happy mood was quickly dispelled by the stern look which Tigh then directed at them.

"There's only one thing worse than lifting rations from the officers' mess," Tigh said, his voice still patient and authoritative. "Do you know what that is, Greenbean?"

"No, sir," Greenbean said, his eyes widening in fear.

"It's getting *caught* lifting rations from the officers' mess. Do I make myself clear?"

All the pilots joined in the subsequent, "Yes, sir!"

"Good. The patrols should return any time now. When Starbuck and Apollo arrive, let's see that things are in full swing."

Tigh's exit was accompanied by a cheer from the pilots. As he took an elevator back to the command bridge, Tigh wondered if he had been presumptive in countermanding the sentries. However, like Adama and all the pilots, he disapproved of the Council's minions. Not only that, the crew, exhausted and overworked as they were, deserved every chance at a short celebration. The bachelor party for Apollo had to take place. That was infinitely more important than a statistical shortage in the officers' mess reports. *Even an old paper-shuffler like me can see that*, he thought.

As he arrived on the bridge, he heard Adama's anxious voice asking a bridge officer:

"Patrol status?"

"Captain Apollo's patrol is still beyond scanning range."

"That's odd," Adama muttered.

Tigh, alerted by the concern in his commander's voice, felt a surge of apprehension. *Apollo had to return*, he thought, *it wouldn't be fair for anything to happen to him now*.

Starbuck racked through the communication channels trying to pick up a response from Apollo. All he received for his frantic efforts were several degrees of crackling static. With his control panel functioning so erratically, he could not even begin to determine the whereabouts of Apollo's ship in the void. Cursing inventively, Starbuck realized there was nothing to do but to enter that hellhole. Well, he'd trusted to luck before. Some said that luck was Starbuck's chief attribute as a fighter pilot.

"Apollo," Starbuck shouted, one last attempt to get a response. "Do you read? Do you read?" The static grew louder and more irritating. "Okay, captain. I'm about to disobey orders. You can testify at my court-martial. So if you want to stop me, I'll give you one last chance, then I'm going to barrel ahead at full turbo, firing my lasers. Sooner or later I'll either find you or we'll both be lost. But I don't cotton to finish off my combat career in the middle of a stupid void, so I'm planning to survive. I have a high survival quotient, all my tests say so. If I do find you, I'm going to execute a perfect one-eighty-degree turn and head back out the way I came in. Just follow me and we'll have a pretty good chance. As good a chance as any other pair of flyboys trapped in a void the likes of which they've never seen before. Now if you're reading me and can't transmit, fire off a laser volley when you see me. I'll know you know what to do. Any objections? Good, I knew you'd approve. Here goes nothing."

Starbuck pressed the joystick button marked TURBO and felt the familiar momentary shudder that preceded the engines kicking in. The stars seemed to blur as his ship roared forward. Entering the void, he was encompassed immediately in darkness. It was as if he had been shoved into a compartment which was then completely sealed off, every crack and vent filled so that not a speck of light could enter. What had possessed him, he thought, thinking he could fly normally in such disorienting darkness. He must concentrate. Concentrate. It was his only chance. He had to keep his viper steady, had to maintain his sense of direction. If he lost that, he could not lead Apollo and himself out of the void. Provided he could find Apollo. Where in all the twelve worlds was he? All Starbuck could see was blackness, not a sign of another spacecraft anywhere. Not a sign of *anything* anywhere. Moving his thumb to the laser-firing button of his joystick, he let off a couple of blasts. They seemed to fade only a short distance away from his craft. Blasting steadily, he barreled his ship forward while simultaneously trying to contact Apollo on the commline. It seemed an impossibly long time before he finally heard Apollo's voice again, slipping through the sounds of interference intermittently.

"Probe . . . *Galactica* . . . Read do you . . . to Starbuck . . . Read . . . Come in . . . buck . . . Star . . ."

Then the voice suddenly came in loud and clear:

"Starbuck, got a scanner reading on you. We're close now. Look off to your, to your left."

Apollo's ship was a black shadow against blackness, but Starbuck could see it. He smiled broadly.

"Okay, probe one. Eye contact verified. Heading your way."

"Starbuck?"

"On my way."

"What's up your sleeve? Now we're both as lost as—"

"Take it easy, Cap'n. As soon as you get a visual on me, fire off a volley and I'll swing around and head straight back out, on one line. Just follow me."

"But what're you using for a fix?"

"The end of my nose. Now don't disorient me. I used to be pretty good at this at the academy. Don't tell anybody, but they used to call me old seat-of-the-pants. So just break off the chatter and get ready to jump on my tail."

Starbuck zeroed in on Apollo's ship. His run at Apollo's viper felt odd. Usually a sweep like this ended in a Cylon ship coming into target range.

"I've got you," Apollo yelled, then fired the volley to signal Starbuck.

"Then follow me. We're going home."

Starbuck, after insuring that Apollo's viper was tight on his tail, headed his own ship back the way—he believed—he had come. As he urged his viper forward, he was aware of the fact that there was no way, in this void, to tell whether or not they were making any progress.

"How far in was I?" Apollo said.

"Don't talk," Starbuck replied.

Starbuck thought the blackness was never going to end. Then, suddenly, he saw a star—a weak low-grade star dimly flickering, but for him it was brighter than the explosion of a supernova. Quickly it was joined by other stars, and he knew they had flown out of the void. He was so happy he felt a sudden urge to pat the seat of his pants for rescuing him again.

"Okay, Apollo. That's one big fat foul cigar you owe me."

"You got it, Starbuck."

"Let's go home, buddy."

As both pilots yelped joyfully, they eased their vipers into a steady roll, executing the maneuver together in perfect textbook fashion.

• • •

Inside Boomer an organism lived, roamed, ate. It did not fit precisely the categories of germ, bacteria, or virus, although it was slowly making Boomer quite sick. It was like nothing humans had ever encountered before on any world. It thrived in moist environments and zeroed in on nutrients like a viper making a run at a Cylon raider. It served no ecological purpose on its world; all it could do was grow and kill. Once it had sensed that Boomer was a harmless nutrient-filled environment, it had entered through the exposed skin of the man's hand. Actually, although Boomer might have cursed himself for removing his gloves, clothing would not have protected him. The organism would have found the treated jumpsuit no obstacle. It went where it wanted to go, anywhere it could carry sickness and death. Another trait of the organism was an ability to multiply itself indiscriminately according to the amount of nutrients available. It sought out new environments eagerly and proliferated. Just before the pilots had climbed back into their ships, it had instantly duplicated itself, and, in a moment when Boomer and Jolly had briefly touched, the duplicate had penetrated Jolly's body. Each pilot now carried a thriving version of the organism inside him. Boomer and Jolly thought they were merely dizzy from overwork, tired from too many patrols.

The lines of Boomer's navigational scan seemed to waver, then do a snakelike dance. He shut his eyes tight for a moment, then opened them to find that the image on the scanner screen had miraculously steadied itself. Still, he could not understand the erratic waves of dizziness that had afflicted him during the flight back from the strange asteroid.

Well, they'd be landing soon and he'd rush through decon and make his report and maybe get to his bunk for some rest. No, not his bunk. There was the party for Apollo first. He mustn't miss that. He owed it to the captain and, anyway, a few sips of ambrosa might just put him right back on his feet.

Flight-control specialist Rigel had Boomer and Jolly hold at the outermarker preparatory to making their landing runs. Through the noises on the commline he could hear Starbuck and Apollo report from further out. *Good,* Boomer thought, *I'll be able to get to the party before the guest of honor. Hate to show up late for this bash.*

"Repeat: Boomer, do you read?"

Repeat? He hadn't heard any previous message from Rigel. Maybe there was some foul-up in the communication system. It was time to overhaul this old viper—way overdue, in fact. It was, after all, one of the originals and not one of those glued-together wrecks that the foundry ships were manufacturing.

"Reading," Boomer said.

"You are cleared to land, Alpha Patrol."

"Thank you."

Boomer didn't know whether what he felt as he aimed his viper toward the landing deck was a wave of relief or another mild bout of dizziness.

"Let's put 'em in, Jolly."

Jolly's ship headed in first. As it neared the pod containing the landing deck, it wavered momentarily from its usual direct line. Boomer was on the commline immediately, shouting:

"Hey, Jolly, get your nose up. I've seen cadets make a better approach than you're making."

Jolly did not respond right away. Boomer became afraid something was wrong. When Jolly finally did speak, it was in a detached, apathetic voice:

"What'd you say just now, Boom—"

"I said, get your nose up and steady up."

Jolly's apparent disorientation and his own feelings of sickness and dizziness made Boomer apprehensive. What could make both of them act so erratically?

"You feel all right, Jolly?"

"I don't know, Boomer. I have a buzzing in my ears." Boomer became conscious of a buzzing in his own ears. "And, I don't know, I feel a little woozy." Boomer felt more than a little woozy. "And cold inside." Boomer's blood seemed to be turning to ice.

"We better get our breather gear checked. When you land—that is, if you land, c'mon, get your nose up, Jolly—when you land, wait for me at the decontamination chamber. Copy?"

"Copy, Boomer."

Somehow Jolly managed a proper landing. Well, proper enough according to the general handbooks, but not the smooth, slick landing one would expect from a pilot of Jolly's skills.

Boomer found it was all he could do to keep his own viper steady as he came in for landing. For a moment after his viper had streaked to a stop, he felt too dizzy to pull himself out of his cockpit. A member of the flight crew offered to help, but Boomer waved the woman away and climbed out unsteadily.

At the decon chamber, Jolly looked about as Boomer felt. His face, normally robust and healthy-looking, was pale and his eyes had clouded over.

"Think we picked up something out there, Boomer?"

"Perhaps. But that's what we have decontamination for. We got anything from that asteroid, we'll get rid of it here."

The organisms, nestled in the bodies of Boomer and Jolly, satisfied their needs indifferently. They might as well be indifferent. The decontamination chamber, keyed to the threats of known microscopic dangers, could not affect them. It could only destroy things whose general nature had been discovered previously. Its scanning did not even detect the presence of the organisms. The organisms, in turn, were not aware of the decon chamber activity. They just went merrily about their business. Well, not merrily, since they had no real awareness of anything, not even of the nutrients they were absorbing.

Boomer convinced himself he felt all right when he came out of decon. He forced his voice to a normal pitch when he reported in by telecom to his commander about their discovery of Cylons on the asteroid.

"A Cylon outpost?" Adama asked.

"Well hidden, but there."

"Thank you, Lieutenant. As usual, the fleet is grateful for your abilities. I'll notify the helm to change course to another quadrant."

"Yes, sir."

As he turned away from the communications console, Boomer knew he should feel content, even a bit happy. He had just received a verbal commendation from his commander—something definitely to feel good about. But good was not what he felt. All he wanted to do right now was climb into his bunk and not respond to a duty call until a superior officer pulled the covers off him and flipped him onto the floor. But first he must do his duty by Apollo, salute the groom-to-be properly and with a rousing ambrosia toast. *Then*, the bunk.

The organism inside Boomer was expanding, duplicating, ready to send out copies of itself into

*other beings. Boomer was about to come in contact
with enough new hosts to relieve any frustration the
organism might have felt, had it been able to feel
frustration.*

Boomer tried to lend his bass-baritone to the
merry song that the other pilots were bellowing, but
he could not. Somehow his voice would not work.
He could not force a single note of music out of it.
Well, no matter. He wasn't the fleet's most eager
singer, anyway. His low notes were usually off-key,
and the high ones were as shaky as a cadet's first
landing.

What he really wanted to do was make a toast,
but to what? Apollo and Starbuck were still in
decon, although it was rumored that their arrival at
the party was imminent. He would have to deliver
some other kind of toast then. Perhaps a general
toast to the success of the fleet, or of the freedom of
pilots everywhere. A freedom being encroached by
the stupid dictates of the Council of Twelve—
maybe he should toast the council, that would have
a proper kind of sarcasm about it. Here's to the
twelve ancients and their jingoistic armed oafs they
choose to legitimize by calling Security Forces. No,
that was too much of a mouthful, and Colonel Tigh
had ordered that they not antagonize the Council at
this time. Maybe a simple "To Life." Yes.

He stood up. He sat down immediately as he
realized how weak and drained his body actually
was.

*Although there was some renewal of nutrient
level, the organism required more, or else it would
go hungry, die along with the host it inhabited.*

Boomer, not one to allow himself to be defeated
easily, forced himself to stand up again, this time
without falling gracelessly back. Getting the attention of the pilots around him, he lifted his glass to

make the toast. Suddenly his fingers would not work, and the glass fell out of his hand, crashing to the floor. Then his legs gave out, and he crashed to the floor, too, narrowly avoiding the shards of broken glass.

"Hey, Boomer."

He looked up. Ensign Giles stared down at him. He could make out the worry on Giles' face through a dense fog that now seemed to be settling into the ready-room. Greenbean's long, lean face appeared over Giles's shoulder.

"Come on," Giles said. "Colonel Tigh's watching us on the monitor."

"Don't clown around," Greenbean said.

"I . . . don't . . . clown," Boomer muttered.

"No, that's right, you don't," Giles said. "Something—"

Tigh's deep voice filled the room:

"With Captain Apollo returning late from patrol, I'd called to extend the curfew under the commander's orders. From what I can see, however, if you men are going to get falling-down drunk . . ."

Boomer, with an effort, sat up and addressed the monitor.

"I'm not drunk, sir. I just got dizzy."

Tigh scowled, obviously not yet ready to believe what was on the surface a pretty lame excuse.

"Any more *dizziness*, and I'll send everyone back to quarters. Understand?"

"Understood!" Greenbean shouted, then whispered to Boomer: "C'mon, I got some special stash that'll make you feel much better. You'll be drunk as a—"

"I . . . don't . . . get . . . drunk."

"Don't talk. You're getting us into enough trouble as it is."

"Hey, I couldn't help it . . . I got . . ."

He tried to stand up again, but his legs wobbled and he faltered. Giles, putting his hands under Boomer's arms, helped him to remain upright.

"Somebody gives Giles and me a hand," Greenbean said. "Sit down and relax, Boomer. You're just tired. Those deep patrols are too long. We all know that."

"It's not that ... It's ... it's ... I can't understand it ... I felt fine after decon ... I felt like ..."

Boomer fell unconscious suddenly. Somebody was going to make another sarcastic remark about how some pilots shamed the code by not being able to hold their ambrosia, when somebody else pointed out that Jolly had just fainted, too.

In the meantime the organism had done rather well. It had made several copies of itself and transmitted them to many new—healthy—hosts.

As he neatly positioned his striped flight helmet in its locker niche, Starbuck realized that his gloomy mood had dissipated. Nothing like meeting a little danger out on patrol to make self-indulgent feelings vanish. In fact, anticipating the bachelor party picked up his spirits immeasurably. Apollo didn't look so happy, however. He looked like a prisoner on the way to an undeserved execution.

"What's the matter, Apollo? You look like you're having the usual second thoughts about getting wed."

"On the contrary, old chum. I feel just fine about the impending ceremony. It's this bachelor party you've cooked up that's frightening me. Maybe I shouldn't go. Maybe—"

"Shouldn't go? You're the guest of honor. You don't even have a choice. I'll drag you there in chains if I have to."

"Well—"

"Well, nothing, Come on, prisoner."

As they entered the corridor leading to the ready-room, Apollo—who had been unusually silent during the long walk, listening sullenly to Starbuck's lively chatter—suddenly said:

"This had better be good. I could be with Serina, you know, and this is delaying an awfully sweet reunion."

"Every time you encounter the least little social obstacle, you start sounding like a country boy fresh off the farm. Apollo, I promise you a night you will long remember."

Starbuck nodded genially to the security man standing guard by the ready-room door, figuring the man had been assigned to see that the frivolity of the party did not spill over into the *Galactica*'s more genteel corridors. There had already been several complaints lodged about pilots' post-combat raucousness from civilians who misunderstood the therapeutic value of such emotional releases. As Starbuck reached for the handle of the ready-room door, the guard spoke brusquely:

"Don't touch the door, skypilot."

Starbuck spun around, ready to battle the guard, who in response gestured menacingly with his left hand while keeping his right hand showily on his holstered laser pistol.

"What's going on? What're—"

"Starbuck! Apollo!" Adama shouted. Starbuck looked back down the corridor. The commander and Colonel Tigh were charging down the passageway, a group of officers keeping pace just behind them.

"Out," Adama ordered, out of breath. "Get out of this corridor. Both of you . . . Colonel, get these men to the bridge."

Tigh gestured Apollo and Starbuck to follow

him. After they had taken a couple of obedient steps, the ready-room door suddenly sprung open. Seeing Boomer being carried by Giles and Greenbean, Starbuck started to move toward his obviously disabled friend.

"Don't get any closer, any of you," warned Doctor Salik, who followed the three men out of the ready-room. Salik was completely covered from head to foot in a transparent decontamination suit.

"I don't know what's wrong here. I don't want any of you to get close to the sick men. You three, who told you to leave the ready-room?"

"Boomer thought if he could just walk around a little . . ."

"Enough! Get back into that room. Guard, send for my staff. We're going to have to transfer everybody attending this party into isolation chambers for study, until I can find out what this is all about. Tell 'em to get the chambers down here as fast as they can. Faster."

The guard rushed off down the corridor.

"Doctor Salik," Apollo said, "what is it? What's happened?"

"I don't know."

"But—"

"Look, I won't speculate. Not my style. I don't even know if this is as bad as it looks."

"Doctor—"

"Forget it, Apollo. I've got to work now."

Realizing there was no further point in interrogating Doctor Salik, who was not an eager talker under normal conditions, Apollo turned to his father.

"What's wrong?"

"I've been afraid of something like this happening. We are just not safe out here, traveling through

sections of the universe we've never seen before. I
think Boomer and Jolly have carried back some
illness from their patrol. A strange virus, perhaps, a
bacterium of some sort. The important thing is that
it seems unknown to us. We have no cures, no
remedies."

"But surely our decontamination procedures
should—"

"They're simply not good enough. We've never
had any guarantee they'd work in all cases. Boomer
and Jolly should have reported their symptoms.
Now they've endangered everybody. Of all the
incredibly stupid—"

"Father, I don't think they can be blamed. If
this—whatever it is—is dangerous, they can't be
expected to think straight in every—"

"Colonial warriors should be expected to think
straight whenever there's the slightest possibility of
danger. I cannot accept excuses."

Apollo, who was often frustrated by his father's
military sternness, decided to check his anger this
time, at least until more became known about the
illness. In the past he and Adama had had long
arguments about what Apollo felt was a too-stiff set
of regulations governing the crew and civilian
passengers of the fleet, but now was not the time for
an analytic discussion of anything. Silently, he
followed Colonel Tigh and Starbuck to the bridge,
where he found the crew performing its duties with
an obvious underlying tension. Adama came on the
bridge a few moments later. He seemed a bit calmer.

"Any news from Salik?" he asked Tigh.

"Only that more of the pilots attending the party
seem to have come down with the illness."

"Keep me posted. The important thing now is to
act on Boomer's information. We've changed

course to avoid a Cylon outpost. That means, Captain Apollo, that we'll be going in along the route explored by you and Starbuck."

"Negative," Apollo said. Adama seemed surprised by the firmness of Apollo's response. "We can't go that way."

"*Can't*? It appears to be the only route we can take now."

"There's something out there that I believe is potentially more dangerous than a Cylon outpost. A magnetic sea, endless, as endless as anything I've ever encountered."

Adama's eyes glazed over pensively as Apollo described the void.

"It was so far across we couldn't scan the other side," Apollo concluded. Adama, his eyes clouding over gradually during Apollo's account of the void, turned abruptly and moved away from his son. He did not even seem to be listening any longer as he walked beside the starfield map. "Father, if you could have seen what it did to my sensors. If Starbuck hadn't flown in after me, I couldn't have made it back, I know that."

"Then that tears it," Tigh said. "We can't go that way. Perhaps there's a way of skirting around the void, follow its perimeter or—what do you think, commander? Commander?"

His face ashen, his eyes still in an apparent daze, Adama turned to Tigh and said:

"I'll be in my quarters. Maintain this course until further orders."

"But we're heading straight for the void, sir. If I may suggest . . ."

"You have your orders, Colonel."

When Adama had left the bridge, walking in a dreamlike slowness, Apollo and Tigh exchanged puzzled, troubled glances, then Tigh ordered the helmswoman to maintain present course and slumped into a command chair.

CHAPTER FOUR

SERINA: I'd just returned from a briefing on emergency procedures to be taken in the event of control-panel malfunction when I heard Boxey delightedly shout out Apollo's name. *Oh God*, I thought, *the moment of truth has come*. I both wanted to see his face and was frightened right out of my wits at the prospect. Quickly, I ran to the mirror to make sure all parts of my outfit were properly in accordance with the service's dress regulations.

Apollo asked Boxey where I was and the boy told him I was in the sleeping quarters. I could hear the laughter in Apollo's voice as he said:

"I'll bet she's trying on her wedding gown and I'm not supposed to see it, right?"

I couldn't figure out what made him jump to that

conclusion. Boxey, who knew my actual outfit, must have provided some clue, a fidgetiness or a fear in his all-too-revealing wide eyes, that told Apollo something was up. It's been pretty tense around here, keeping secrets from my own fiancé.

"Apollo, I'll be right out," I hollered.

He shouted back that I was not to worry, he didn't think it bad luck to see the bride in her gown before the wedding day. I was tempted to protest, use that ancient prenuptial superstition as a convenient excuse to postpone the confrontation, then I decided it was better to get it all over with, so I told him to come in.

When Apollo saw me (trying to appear elegant in my best high-fashion pose), he looked so stunned I thought for a moment he might actually be liking it. I mean, it *was* the first time he'd seen me in my cadet's uniform, after all.

I tried to make it easier for him by saluting, hoping that an exaggerated militariness might at least amuse him. He always says he likes the satiric approach.

"Flight Cadet Serina, reporting for duty, Captain," I said in my best clipped, warriorlike voice. I had been imagining this moment for a long time, knowing he would be shocked to see me in the brown buckskin jacket and close-fitting trousers. I'd believed that, after a moment of astonishment, he would be happy to see it.

"What is this? A joke?" he said angrily.

I was so disappointed, I couldn't answer at first.

"No. I just wanted to surprise you. I've been in flight training ever since your father opened up the program to replace the pilots we've lost."

"Training!" he shouted. "You've been training to—"

"I'm a shuttle cadet, Apollo. I've soloed. My

evaluation reports are good, they're—"

"Boxey, would you excuse us a moment?"

Boxey was peeved at being dismissed from the conversation. He'd been watching us as if we were performing a little comedy just for his benefit. Looking down at his daggit, he muttered:

"Come on, Muffit. They're going to argue."

"We are not going to argue," I said, as firmly as I could under the circumstances.

"Yes, they are," Boxey said to Muffit, as he closed the door behind him.

"Yes, we are!" Apollo vowed, and I knew I had a real fight on my hands.

No matter, I thought, *I can handle it.* At least I hoped I could. Looking at the wrath in my betrothed's face, I was no longer so sure.

"You didn't even tell me!" Apollo said. "That's what hurts the most. I was not even good enough for—"

"Come off it, darling. You know why I didn't tell you. I wouldn't've seen the inside of a cockpit if I'd so much as mentioned—"

"All right. I'll concede the point. I'm an arrogant, browbeating martinet who can't be trusted to consider both sides of a matter like this. All right, I—"

"Stop that. There's no need to go highside about it. If I was wrong in not telling you, I'm sorry, but—"

"No one told me. Of all the—I'm supposed to be the Flight Commander, remember? I still haven't even received a single report on our little makeshift flight academy. Does my father know you're—"

"No. He doesn't get a report on every cadet in the fleet."

Apollo looked ready to flunk the whole fleet on an efficiency report. He also looked very, very angry. I wanted to reach out and touch him, but I was afraid he might not take too kindly to even a mild expression of affection at that precise moment. Finally, the words coming out like bursts of laser fire, he said:

"It's . . . it's too dangerous. I can't . . . I won't . . ."

I realized suddenly that I, too, was very angry.

"You don't have a choice!" I shouted.

It was not sensible to fight him like that—with foolish bluffs, especially—for, after all, he did have a choice. As flight commander and son of Adama, he could get me tossed off mission roster easily. My approach should have been to soothe him but instead, impulsive squabbler that I am, I had responded in kind.

"Serina, it's not—not right. It's—"

"Not right? For what reason?"

"We're about to be married!"

I should have expected that. So many of the males aboard this battlestar think that just dropping the words "married," "marriage," "wedding," "wife" into a conversation automatically defines the issue. Once the words build the fences, they think, there should be no arguments. Well, that might have worked with some women, but I'd had too much independence for too long back on Caprica, and I wasn't about to let Apollo try to make gender a defining principle.

"Yes, we're about to be married, but what does that have to do with it? Your own sister's a pilot—and warrior!"

"She's my sister. Not my wife-to-be!"

"Well, if that's all that's disturbing you, we can take care of that. Easily. I'll be just another cadet and you won't have to worry about it. I always knew I didn't believe in marriage contracts. Now I see why!"

Apollo is nothing if not a good officer. He knew when to retreat by being forward. He put his arms around me and said:

"Serina, I love you. That's what counts. I don't want anything to happen to you, ever."

Acknowledging his calmness, I regained control over my own emotions.

"Don't you think I love you, too?" I said. "And talking about danger, look at things from my point of view. You're always going off on patrols, flying missions in a viper. Into combat. And don't hand me any of your bilge about the viper being the most efficient and successful war machine ever developed. I've seen too many of them go down launch tube for the last time to buy that line. And I'm not even attempting to qualify as a viper pilot. Kobol forbid. All I'm training to be, after all, is a shuttle pilot."

"Do you know how many shuttle pilots have been picked off by Cylon sneak attacks, how many shuttle pilots were lost at the Battle of Carillon?"

"Do you know how many civilians? Apollo, face it, there is no really safe place or job-function anywhere in the fleet. That's why we need the emergency procedures so desperately. Everyone is being trained in every capacity. It's our best chance for survival."

"Yes, but—"

But he couldn't come up with any more buts. He glanced away from me as if studying the gray rows of rivets in the metal wall panels, then back at me. Then he sighed, then he let out a breath. Finally he said:

"Are you any good?"

"Top of my class."

He pulled me closer.

"You better be if you're going to be married to a squadron commander."

"Oh, well, then . . . Yes, sir."

He kissed me then. And—for the moment—that particular battle was over. A standoff followed by a truce and time to regroup.

I'm sorry, in a way, that we had to go through the pattern of anger and conciliation. I've never had a chance to tell him how scared I am, how I can't sleep nights for fear of dreams in which a Cylon raider bears down on me and shoots off a laser blast that surrounds me in blinding whiteness before I wake up. I told Athena about my uneasy dreams. She just passed them off, called them cadet sweat.

But the dreaming doesn't stop.

CHAPTER FIVE

Cassiopeia walked down the aisle between the double row of support chambers, checking the gauges on each to see that the proper cryonic levels were being maintained. She stopped at Boomer's chamber for a long while, trying to see a flicker of life on the young man's face. The rime frost which had collected on the inside of the chamber's glass gave Boomer a ghostly look. Although all measuring instruments indicated that he lived, there was no sign of life on his face. For that matter, all of the men seemed encased in their coffins rather than in life-support devices.

A shudder seemed to go through her entire body as she momentarily envisioned Starbuck sealed in one of the life-support tubes. When he had told her how close he had come to charging by the security guard and entering the party room, he had been blasé about it, as if this mysterious sickness could not touch him. Still, *everyone* at that party was now down with the illness. Further, one pilot had left the party on the trail of amatory adventure. He had collapsed before he'd annoyed any passing woman, but he'd made contact with several members of the security force who had made contact with others and, at the moment, there was no telling how far this plague might spread. If the quarantine procedures and stiffer curfew regulations did not work, then anyone—Starbuck, Apollo, Serina, the commander—could contract the disease. No new cases had been reported for two duty-tours, so Doctor Salik believed the communicable phase might be in check now. But, as he said, how could anyone predict the progress of a disease no one knew anything about? Tears welled up in her eyes as she thought of Starbuck, and fervently hoped that he would be able to goldbrick himself off the duty roster to be with her after her own tour of duty ended. She wanted to hold him, protect him even while he protested he needed no protection. Maybe she could get him to stay with her for an entire rest period instead of rushing off to some game table somewhere. (Where? All his gambling buddies were here, planted in life-support tubes.) If only he'd stay—maybe if she bet him eight to five that he wouldn't . . .

Doctor Salik, who had been working with the ship computer, feeding in all known data and receiving inconclusive responses, suddenly turned away from the console and interrupted her thoughts of Starbuck by muttering:

"Still nothing. I've put in all that I know about their symptoms, eliminated everything that's tested out negative. There's no more I can come up with."

"But we—"

"Let's go over it again. Review the symptoms."

This was the tenth time, at least, that he had asked Cassiopeia for a recital of symptoms. Each time she dutifully provided it:

"Dizziness. Rapid pulse. Sudden fainting spells. Fever. Lowering blood cell count. That's most of them."

"I know, I know. And I still haven't got a clue. Everybody in the fleet could die and I'll still be here getting inconclusives from the computer."

She put her hand on his arm. The skin around his eyes had grown so puffy, the eyes themselves seemed to be hiding behind battlements.

"Take it easy, doctor."

"Right, Cassie. I just don't—"

He stopped talking when he realized that the *Galactica*'s commander now stood on the other side of Boomer's tubelike chamber. The man had entered the life-support station so silently that neither doctor nor med-tech had taken note of him.

"I just got a report," Adama said. "This disease swept through every fighter pilot and half the bridge officers. Everyone who came in contact with anyone who'd been at the party. Clearly it originated with Jolly and Boomer. Decon chamber checked out as fully operative."

"I've taken dozens of scans of the bodies of the infected pilots, sir. Nothing indicated. Nothing bacteriological or viral at any rate. Something's happening to their blood and there's a definite weakening of the intestinal tract, but these and other symptoms don't add up to anything I can work with. Whatever is causing this, I can't isolate it. I can only leave the men in cryogen tubes until we do get closer to a solution. Jolly and Boomer would be dead now if I hadn't put them into cryogenic suspension. And I'd guess that that's only delaying the inevitable unless I can isolate the source of infection. And soon."

Cassiopeia had never seen such distress in the commander's face before. She remembered Tigh describing to her Adama's reaction to viewing the explosion of his young son Zac's viper at the inception of the Cylon diversionary ambush. Adama must have looked then as he did now, ready to break down and cry at any moment.

"Doctor," Adama said, "do you understand the significance of these men? These particular men? They've been overworking themselves daily, protecting the fleet. We can't afford to lose them now."

Salik, clearly holding in his temper, inhaled deeply before replying:

"I understand all that, Commander. But I have to say with all due respect that the problems of defense are yours. My job right now is keeping them alive."

Adama, less successful at checking his temper, shouted:

"Do your job then, doctor!"

Salik's voice lowered as he said:

"As soon as you stop looking over my shoulder every few moments, Commander, I'll do my job."

Both men appeared to Cassiopeia as if they could come to blows the next time one of them spoke. They were silent, fortunately, for a long moment, then Adama whirled on his heels and strode out of the life-support station. Salik did not bother to look after the commander, but instead returned to the computer console to feed into it the same information he had been giving it since the first symptoms had been diagnosed.

Starbuck, Cassiopeia thought, *you better be there tonight. I need you.*

• • •

Adama, still feeling rankled from his confrontation with Salik, sought solace by examining again
the microfilmed pictures of the ancient books of
Kobol. He stopped particularly at an old map to
study it. The lovely calligraphy of the map was
written in the ancient language, very little of which
was translatable. It appeared to show a bright
shining star in a circle with long, snakelike rays
shooting out from its center. And the large
oceanlike area funneling out from the planet
certainly might be a representation of what Apollo
and Starbuck had described as the void. One of the
alternate translations for the mysterious inscription
below the oceanlike area seemed to describe a vast
void stretching across an entire galaxy. If they went
inside it, and its pull delivered them to that star and
that planet, why then—

"You sent for me, father."

He had not heard Apollo enter. Looking at the
young man now, he started to smile. However, he
had to suppress his paternal instinct when he
perceived how angry Apollo looked. The welcoming smile quickly diminished.

"Yes, Apollo. I had Colonel Tigh prepare a roster
of everyone in the fleet with any flight experience."

The roster lay on a corner of Adama's desk. He
picked it up and handed it to his son, who seemed
reluctant to accept it.

"Basically," Adama continued, "it comes down
to a small number of combat-trained pilots, then a
larger group of old-line warriors with disabilities of
one kind or another. Plus those names at the
bottom."

Holding the roster away from him as if it were
particularly distasteful, Apollo squinted down at

the names upon it. When he reached the bottom group of names, he inhaled sharply and muttered:

"Oh, no."

"Those last names," Adama said, "are those cadets who have had some solo experience, although none of them have so much as touched a viper joystick. Get them combat-ready as soon as possible."

Apollo gripped the roster so tightly that crumple lines appeared in the paper all around his hand.

"You're not serious?" he said, quite angrily.

What is this? Adama thought. *Everybody's spoiling for an argument today, it seems. First Salik, now Apollo, each ready to explode at me.*

"I'm quite serious," Adama said firmly, hoping that would put his son's argument to rest.

"Father," Apollo said, "the viper is an extremely complicated piece of machinery. It's designed to integrate tightly with the skills of a pilot. I sometimes feel it would chuck me right out of the cockpit if it decided it could do without me. You can't just assign vipers to . . . to shuttle pilots. It's—"

"We don't know how long it'll be before our sick pilots can return to combat. Or if they'll ever be able to. We can't wait. That's how serious I am; that's how serious the situation is. I don't mean to be brusque, but I am busy." He glanced irritably toward the antiquated map on his viewer. "You have your orders."

"Yes sir, but—"

"What is it?"

Apollo slapped the roster list back onto Adama's desk and walked briskly to the door, where he turned and said quietly:

"I just don't believe you read all the names on that roster, Commander."

After Apollo had shoved open the compartment

door and charged out of the room, Adama slowly picked up the roster from where Apollo had thrown it down. Looking at the bottom names, he saw immediately what had angered his son. Serina was listed as one of the qualified shuttle pilots. Too busy with the many details of command, Adama had not before realized that Serina had gone through on her threat to take pilot training. He recalled the day when she'd announced her intention, and he had impolitely scoffed, saying that her duty was to be Apollo's helpmate. What had she said then, her voice nearly shrill with indignation? Something to the effect that an individual's duty had to include more than a simple-minded commitment to another individual, especially for reasons that had become outmoded with the first Cylon burst of fire in the attack on the twelve worlds. Curbing his anger and struggling to take a conciliatory approach, Adama had tried to talk her out of the idea of becoming a pilot, saying she could be more useful helping the sick or overseeing supplies or, with her talents in that direction, participating in food preparation. Although she clearly saw his suggestions as condescending, she had not argued with him about them. On the other hand, she had not agreed with him either.

Now he could not avoid ordering her to risk her life. He could not excuse her from duty and then send out other eligible but just as inexperienced pilots.

"Oh, lord," Adama muttered, not knowing exactly what he would say to his son the next time they met.

Cassiopeia nestled her head in Starbuck's shoulder and sang one of the songs she remembered from her socialator days. Fleet Council had

banished the practice of socialation, among other
luxury occupations, as inimical to the goals of
eluding Cylon pursuit and seeking Earth. She had
pushed memories of her earlier life out of her mind.
However, she had never been able to forget
completely the music. It was, after all, lovely,
especially so since it had been composed to treat
specific emotional problems. The song she now
sang, "The Death That Is No Death, the Life That Is
All Life," seemed particularly appropriate to
Starbuck's mood. He was afraid for Boomer and his
other comrades, all lying in that bizarre coma in life
station. After a moment of listening to Cassiopeia's
soft and haunting voice, he put his arm around her
and brought her closer to him. Cassiopeia finished
her song and then the two enjoyed the silence. The
relative silence, anyway—there was no possibility of
total silence inside the busily functioning *Galactica*.

"If you feel like a smoke, go ahead," Cassiopeia
finally said.

Starbuck smiled and whispered:

"Nope. I know how you hate the smell of my
cigars even when they're made from the slickest and
most potent tobacco found on Sagitara. Boomer
saved some from—"

He stopped talking abruptly. His and Boomer's
lives were so complexly intertwined that it seemed
he could not speak on a subject without somehow
bringing Boomer into it. Cassiopeia cursed silently.
There was nothing, it seemed, in all her socialator
training—all the complex arts, devices, theories,
intended to help a woman administer to her male
clients—that countered the gloom caused by the
closeness of death, not even the soft, sad songs.

"Starbuck, do you wish—"

"I have to go, Cassie."

"No, please stay."

"I'm not good company—"

"That doesn't matter."

"Well, I've got to be in good shape to ogle all my pupils in the new flight-training classes tomorrow."

"That sounds a bit like the Starbuck I'm used to, I'll admit that. But I don't believe it. You're just—"

"Cassie, I have to be alone for a while."

"Be alone with me."

"I can't. You're wonderful, Cass, but—"

"It's a standoff then."

"Not exactly. I'm going."

"Starbuck, please—"

Delicately, he removed his arm from around her waist and disengaged himself.

"I'm jealous, you know," Cassiopeia muttered.

Some of the sadness left Starbuck's face. Her jealousy pleased him, as she knew it would.

"Jealous? Why?"

"You and Athena. You'll be together all during classes, all during—"

Starbuck roared with laughter.

"I can see you don't know Athena very well. When it comes to something like this, anything tinged with the odor of duty, she's all business. No reason at all for you to be jealous."

"But you do, I take it, allow for jealousy outside of duty situations?"

"Don't try to catch me out. I'm yours forever, or until, or if. That's the best I can ever promise you."

She suppressed saying, "Or any other woman." This was not the time for that kind of sardonic remark. Starbuck touched her cheek with the back of his hand, then left the room suddenly. She watched the door for a long time, hoping to see him return.

• • •

Gemi was a short, young woman, standing at least an inch below the colonial-service height requirement. By smiling pertly and distracting the inspector, she was able to stand on her toes and be qualified. Although her vision was subpar, she parlayed a secret squint with a good memory to pass the eye test. She had an odd, hereditary nervous disease, common only to natives of Gemon, her home planet, which in periods of stress could cause her fingers to tremble uncontrollably. She told none of the examining doctors about it. She had a talent for taking tests, and she was able to pass the pilot qualifier even though she understood fewer than half the questions. She should not have been accepted for training as a viper pilot replacement, but nobody knew that, since she had tricked and conned her way through all the preliminary screenings. They might have taken her provisionally anyway. Anyone who wanted to be a pilot that badly deserved special treatment—Gemi thought so anyway.

The only matter that troubled her at all was that she could not figure a way to attract Lieutenant Starbuck's attention. She knew it was ridiculous to have a crush on the dashing and popular young officer but, for her, affairs of the heart had never followed accepted logic. Her chief obstacle to amatory success was that so many of the ladies had fallen for Starbuck that she was already lost in the crowd. The worst irony for all the female cadets in the new viper piloting classes was that Starbuck, defying his notoriety as fabled womanizer, had turned into an all-business instructor and was not giving any of the girls a tumble. In her moments of despair Gemi felt that he'd never notice her, not with all the competition. What would he see in her tiny, heart-shaped face?, she thought. Her chin came to too sharp a point and her forehead was much too wide. If only she had been blessed with the kind of wide blue eyes that men so annoyingly notice. Instead, her eyes were small and a dull brown. Her facial lacks might have been salvaged if she could have presented a slimly attractive figure, but hers was compact and chunky, the kind of sturdy body that was good for playing a tough game of triad or riding a wild mount, but not the silly sort of curvaceous frame that titillated men. Although she was reasonably successful in the love wars that occupied so much of the nonbattle time aboard the ships of the fleet, she was discouraged that she too often had to settle for swains whose standards of ethical conduct were not always acceptable to her, or for that matter to any woman who could assemble a set of two or three standards for her own use. The men of the fleet were not always, as she might have put it, representative of the ideal in human life. Far from it.

She set her cap for Starbuck anyway. The first day of training she asked every question she could think of, until the rest of the class groaned every time she held up her hand. But no matter how perceptive or well-phrased her question, Starbuck answered in an occupied manner, hardly ever looking away from his clipboard at her. His indifference to her intellectual display would not have been so irksome if he had not been willing to banter after class with every other female—at least, every tall, well-formed, pretty female—in the class.

Well, she vowed, if intelligence didn't catch his eye, she'd try skill, and she began to apply her considerable energies and talents to becoming an adept pilot. Perhaps, she thought, the way to a man's heart is through his viper.

CHAPTER SIX

SERINA: I'm so all-out exhausted I don't even know if I'll be able to finish this report. Anybody who thinks training to be a combat pilot is the least bit romantic is welcome to take my place in cadet class. At this point I've been shot down so many times in simulated battles that, what with the numbness in *all* my muscles, I am beginning to think I really am dead. I can't quite master the knack of shooting off laser fire in conjunction with the accelerative thrust of the viper. My thumb on the joystick just doesn't make the proper instinctive moves in the correct rhythm. Athena says it's tough for all beginners. You've got to act before you can actually think of the action itself, she says. She runs a tough drill, but I think I'm learning. Still, I keep thinking I'll never really get the hang of it. Not really. Not that feel a real pilot gets when everything's buzzing and the ship skims like a sailboat. I've got to get it. If only to prove something to Apollo.

Apollo.

Really, he's been awfully sweet about everything. Yet—ever since training began I haven't been able to lose the feeling that he's always on my neck, hovering. I mean, he doesn't scream or criticize, and he really does try to help. Everybody adores him as a teacher. I just can't get rid of this dumb suspicion that he actually *wants* me to fail. It's hard to explain sensibly. He's proud, I know, when I do well in the classroom. (I've really proven to be much better at theory than combat practice.) But at the same time his pride is, I don't know, *tinged* in some way. While he takes some pride in my doing well, what he actually wants is for me to be safe here in my compartment on the *Galactica*, without any thoughts of lasers or vipers to interfere with my bridely perceptions. I mean, it's sweet really. He is not the sort of man who feels threatened by a woman's competition. At least I don't think so. He's just so caring that he doesn't want anything to happen to me, and no amount of arguing that it's for the good of the fleet can sway him. After all, he's a hero of the fleet. He knows he accomplishes enough for two and that no one would really blame him if he exerted command influence to ban me from all cockpits. Still, I'd like to show him. I'll never be as good a pilot as he is, I'm sure, but at least I can be a damn good pilot and that's what's important to me now. God, I never thought that the biggest thing in my life would become whether or not I could develop the skills to hold my ship on a steady course.

The warrior I'd sometimes like to strangle is Starbuck. The man is incorrigible, I swear. Watching him supervise training, you'd think he'd achieved the major dream of his life. Maybe he has. Certainly he's never had this many women at his command before. And scuttlebutt has it that, before training, he held the record for holding women at his command. But now—*now* he's really in his element; after each session, he zooms from female cadet to female cadet. It can be really annoying sometimes, although I must admit that most of the young cadets seem to enjoy it immensely.

That first day, when we were issued our uniforms, Starbuck was everywhere, adjusting straps, dusting insignia, straightening sleeves. He kept muttering how glad he was to be able to lend a hand. Dietra muttered to me that he seemed even gladder to lend *two* hands. He seems particularly eager to help out a cute little blonde named Brie. She's a transfer from *Rising Star*, the former luxury liner, some of whose facilities have been useful for fleet R & R. Rumor has it she was a hostess in one of its many lounges when the Cylon attack came. She can't seem to do anything right. During G-suit drill, she kept trying to fasten her pressure strap below her knee instead of above. Wouldn't you know, there was Starbuck, smirking at her and telling her it wouldn't do much good down there. Well, Brie gave him her wide-eyed little-girl look and he volunteered to readjust it for her. What he wanted to do in the first place, I expect. He made it look good. As he slid the strap over her knee and began to tighten it—taking his time, of course—he explained in proper academy voice that it was an electronic pressure pad designed to help her body withstand the enormous forces of rapid acceleration and deceleration.

Athena's furious with him, of course. Cassiopeia would be, too, if she weren't so busy at the life

support station. Whenever Starbuck's around Brie
or one of the others, Athena's usually watching him,
even while attending to her teaching responsibilities
efficiently. She has become quite adept at maneuvering herself between Starbuck and his momentary objects of attention. In a way, their rivalry
has been good for the rest of us. They compete, try
to outdo each other in their sections of practice, and
we all learn from their sharpened concentration.
Yesterday Athena beat Starbuck out in a simulated
target run, and he said she'd been lucky—she'd
started the run too early and, by all rights, should
have so mis-timed her shot that it ought to have
missed the target by a mile instead of splitting it into
a million electronic bits. She kept her cool and
merely replied that maybe her timing had been, well,
anticipatory, but in this particular run her mis-
timing had saved him from being blasted out of the
skies. He challenged her judgment, and they went to
computer for settlement. The replay of the practice
run, which analyzed each move and manipulation
of the pilots, showed that Athena had been right.
Her timing had saved Starbuck from a probable
pinwheel attack from the simulated Cylon ships,
one in which his chances for survival were not at all
good. One thing I'll say for Starbuck, he may go
after women with an annoying predictability, but he
is not afraid to admit his errors. He was quite
gracious in admitting before the class that Athena
had won the challenge. There are times, especially
when I notice a sad cast to Starbuck's eyes, that I
believe his exuberance is a kind of compensation for
his worries about Boomer.

When Apollo was giving us the lecture about the
pressure suit, explaining in detail the G-force
differences between shuttle and viper flight, he
caught my eye. I had, after all, placed myself right in

front of his lectern. I formed the words, I love you, and pantomimed them in his direction. He got very red, and nobody else knew why. I enjoyed that. Later, when we were in the simulator, he sneaked up behind me and put his arms around me, said loudly that I was overcontrolling and should relax—hold the stick lightly, lightly. Then he leaned in to whisper:

"I love you, too."

Sometimes the training is worth it, after all. But, God, I do hope I can get the hang of those controls before I have to take a real viper onto patrol. I wish I—I'm too tired to continue, I think I'm going to fall asleep right now. Serina, signing off and nodding off.

CHAPTER SEVEN

Lucifer was finding it extremely difficult to keep his real self submerged under the overlay personality. He did not like maintaining a subservient attitude to Baltar, and especially detested having to suppress his commentaries about his commander's observations and opinions.

Accompanied by a Cylon warrior, especially detached to guard him, Lucifer glided into the command room. As usual, Baltar, sitting in the pedestal throne, faced the wall. To get his attention, Lucifer said:

"By your command."

Slowly the command chair swung around and Baltar peered down at him. Was he mistaken or did Baltar's mouth now show distinct signs of contempt? The man became more difficult to deal with daily.

"Yes, Lucifer? What little astronomical deviation or minor course adjustment constitutes your excuse to interrupt my meditational period this time?"

The man was beginning to talk like a tyrant. Meditational period, indeed. Baltar was not capable of the kind of meditation that an imperious leader achieved. Not long ago he had been dispatched to a garbage chute; now he was becoming a full-fledged demigod.

"I am sorry, the interruption is necessary. We have overtaken the *Galactica* and are trailing just beyond her scanner range."

Baltar chuckled softly.

"Excellent."

"She has now veered away from the outpost asteroid."

"Ah, yes, I anticipated that."

"Certainly, on the face of it, it is not illogical. But their course is taking them into the Epsilon quadrant toward a magnetic abyss."

First Baltar studied Lucifer's face silently, then abruptly he stood up and looked off toward his left, roughly in the direction of Epsilon quadrant.

"A magnetic abyss? It couldn't be. Describe please."

"A void, a navigational inferno. Our equipment does not reveal its dimensions, it could possibly be endless. It seems to me that, given the opportunity to proceed toward the abyss or to engage our forces at the outpost, they should have chosen the outpost."

"Perhaps they know we are following, and the move toward the abyss is diversionary."

"Anything is possible, but the odds—as I've computed them—seem astronomically against that possibility. I don't think we have been detected and their movement toward the abyss seems purposeful. Shall we launch our fighters against the *Galactica* now?"

Baltar sat again in the command throne, put his hand up to his chin. Lucifer had to admit to himself that the man feigned meditation better than he might have expected.

"No," Baltar finally said. "They do too well in open space. We have to get them confined, trapped in a corner. We'll wait. Have they sent out reconnaissance patrols?"

"On occasion. They have tended to patrol forward and we have managed to drop back beyond the scanner range of rear patrols."

Baltar nodded.

"That's it then. That's what we'll do."

Lucifer noted that Baltar, as always, was quite adept at stating the speculative as if it were factual.

"Give top priority to capturing one of those patrol pilots. If what I suspect is true, and Adama is off on this particular futile quest, then there is a definite chance we might get him to turn the *Galactica* over to us without firing a shot. All that is necessary is that I play the psychological part of the game efficiently. That will be all, Lucifer."

"By your command."

As he left, Lucifer remarked to himself that Baltar had a certain exploitable talent for the devious, all right. The only trouble was, he was so devious, even those on his side could not figure out what he was up to. For the moment, Baltar's fancy-stepping was useful, but it might have to be dealt with differently at a later time.

Adama tried to make sense out of the void as it was now displayed on the central scanner screen. He wished it could really be seen and analyzed. But how

could one see and analyze emptiness? All he could
see were stars surrounding the immense blackness.
Any analysis was speculative, dangerously speculative.

Tigh, clutching a readout, came to his side.

"Long-range scanners cannot detect an end to
it," he reported. "It could be infinite."

"No, not infinite, Colonel. I doubt that strongly."

Tigh, clearly uncertain of whether or not his
commander was mentally and emotionally stable,
furled his brow and gave the documents to a
crewman. Doctor Salik, rubbing his hands together
as if to ward off any disease that might have
infiltrated the bridge, approached Adama.

"Doctor," Adama said, without looking up,
"how soon can we expect our pilots to be returned to
duty?"

Salik's stare at Adama was, if anything, a shade
less encouraging than Tigh's. Clearly both men were
concerned about their leader's sanity.

"Commander," Salik said, "two more men just
went critical. I'm going to have to stack life support
chambers in the corridors if this keeps up. So it's not
a question of how soon they'll be back on duty, it's a
question of how soon they'll die."

Salik scowled at both men, a characteristic look
for the overworked doctor, then he said in a lower
voice:

"I want permission to return to wherever those
two lieutenants landed. If I can isolate the source of
the infection—"

"Negative, doctor," Tigh said. "That asteroid's
behind us and has a Cylon sentinel post. There's no
way we can risk any more personnel on that
godforsaken place, especially with so many dangerous contingencies."

"But if we don't—"

"I appreciate your situation, doctor, but you must realize that, with most of our experienced pilots down with this disease, we cannot provide you with sufficient trained personnel to form a proper escort. It would be suicide to send out the personnel we have now."

"Forget the escort personnel. My team and I'll take the chance. It's vital we—"

"I'm impressed by your willingness to take such a risk, Doctor Salik," Adama interrupted. "But Colonel Tigh is right. I can't permit such a mission, even for such vital research purposes. Not without proper escort."

Tears came into Doctor Salik's eyes as he pleaded:

"Commander, going back there is the only hope those boys have. The only hope!"

The word *hope* struck a responsive chord in Adama's breast. It was a word that had, after all, become something of a litany with him, a word he retreated to when all the other words were failing. The doctor may have invoked it with calculation, a desperate last-moment measure to support another desperate last-moment measure, but Adama knew he must give the doctor his due. A large measure of command responsibility rested in the ability to listen and respond to the judgment of other trusted professionals.

"You're certain of that, doctor?"

"I stake all my professional experience on it, Commander."

Adama turned away from the doctor, glanced again at the image of the void on the screen, then turned to Communications Lieutenant Omega.

"What's the present status, updated, of Blue Squadron?"

"Simulator training continuing. Third-level

combat situations being tried. First solos in viper already completed."

"How are the proficiency ratings of the new cadets?"

"Surprisingly high, sir."

Glancing back at Salik, he said:

"All right, doctor. So be it. You have your mission. Select and prepare a medical team, then report back to me."

The doctor nodded matter-of-factly and left the bridge. Salik was not one to offer effusive thanks when he got his way. Tigh moved toward Adama, questioning his commander's decision with a worried look.

"Let's hope and pray those cadets are ready," Adama said. "Call Captain Apollo to the bridge."

Involuntarily Adama hunched his shoulders. Perhaps, he thought, his body was anticipating the angry words that would come from his son.

Apollo, sitting in the simulator room observation booth, felt as if he had been cast out into deep space when the lights went down and the starfield clicked on. Even though he knew that the vipers were only partial models and that most of the ships zooming across his line of sight were in actuality small models being projected into the holographic combat simulation from another booth across the way, he found the illusion quite persuasive. He remembered his first sessions in such a simulation field. When fake laser fire had come right at his face, it had been so realistic he had thought for a brief moment that he'd been killed.

Athena ran the present session. Her voice magnified by loudspeakers, she sounded like a tough drill sergeant. She was certainly taking no nonsense from Brie and Dietra, the pair of cadets

currently in the simulation-field. She barked out
orders and criticized their performance mercilessly.
Brie, a blonde-haired youthful woman, appeared to
take every rebuke to heart, while Dietra, a
dark-skinned wiry type, displayed nothing but a
seasoned cynicism on her face, no matter what
Athena said.

"Keep your tails up, ladies.... Easy on the
joystick, Dietra. It's not a club to beat Starbuck's
head in, it's a delicate, sensitive device.... Check
your scanner, Brie.... No, no, to your left and
down.... That's better.... Good move, Dietra....
Okay, let's heat it up!"

Apollo very much enjoyed watching his sister run
the drill like this. On the other hand, Starbuck,
squirming in the next seat, did not seem to derive
any pleasure at all from his observation, perhaps
because Athena invoked his name so often as a
target for the cadets to shoot at.

Simulations of Cylon raiders appeared without
warning behind the viper-models of Dietra and
Brie. Dietra immediately set her mock-vehicle into a
rolling maneuver, leaving Brie apparently alone and
vulnerable for a moment before she copied Dietra's
move.

"Stay on Dietra's tail, Brie.... That's good
.... Here they come!"

The illusory battle of half-ships and shadow-thin
attackers was short and sweet. After sweeping away
from their marauders, Brie got off a pair of shots
that, as the sensory information from the chargeless
laser reached the collection of dots that were the
Cylon craft, caused the raiders apparently to
explode.

"I did it!" Brie screamed, her eyes aglow with joy.
"I did it! I did it!"

There was a long pause before Athena responded

in a voice that sounded like her father giving a subordinate due sarcasm:

"You sure did, Brie. You not only got the Cylons, you got Dietra, too."

"What?"

"After blasting the Cylons, you crossed Dietra's tail while still firing. She's dead."

Dietra managed a weak acknowledging smile and looked sympathetically in Brie's direction.

"I'm sorry," Brie murmured.

"*You're* sorry," Dietra said, and rolled her eyes upward.

Everybody laughed and the simulator scene was switched off. Apollo was about to direct a new test, when the ship intercom loudspeaker blared:

"Captain Apollo, please report to Commander Adama on the bridge. On the double."

Apollo switched on the observation booth mike and said:

"Have to jump. Athena, take Brie through another session and see if we can arrange everybody's survival."

"Right. Okay, Brie, this one's for the money."

He found his father and Tigh staring at the approaching void on a monitor. There was an air of gloom hanging about both men.

"Commander," Apollo said.

Adama, his eyes cold and distant, turned and said:

"How are the cadets doing?"

Apollo felt tense inside. His father could still scare him—with a hard glance or a stern question— even after the years of serving together.

"They're doing fine, sir, considering the closest they've been to a viper previously was probably at an Armament Day display."

"According to their grades and ratings, this

group of cadets is doing almost as well as an honors class at the academy."

Apollo shrugged.

"Figures lie, father. We don't have the equipment or personnel to qualify for a proper academy rating. Our tests are not thorough. Our measurements are only as good as the personnel interpreting them, which is to say not very good. Against these limitations, the figures are encouraging."

"Which means, if I understand correctly, that they are about as combat-ready as we, with our limited resources, are able to make them."

"I didn't mean that at all. I—"

"Nevertheless that's the meaning I must put upon the data you've provided me."

"But—"

"We can't wait any longer, Captain."

Adama strode directly to his son. To Tigh, the anger in both men's eyes appeared to be a matched set.

"Doctor Salik has requested a medical team," Adama said, "to be sent back to the asteroid where Boomer and Jolly apparently contracted this disease. He feels it's his only chance to gain the information needed to arrive at a cure."

"Surely you don't endorse such a plan. It's liable to be a one-way mission. What about the Cylon post—"

"I suggest we send a squadron as an escort."

The full import of the commander's statement settled onto Apollo slowly. He really meant it. This was not just a discussion. He intended to send out the mission and a squadron to accompany it!

"It's precisely for that reason, sir, that the mission is not possible. There are not enough experienced pilots to—Father! No, you can't mean that. There's no way those cadets can do it. Most of

them haven't logged more than solo time in a real
viper. Sure, considering their experience, or lack of
it, they're doing quite well. But they're a long way
from being able to fly a mission! It's too risky."

Adama turned away from his son, glanced again
at the void on the monitor.

"Everything we do has an element of risk,
Apollo. You're a risk-taker yourself."

"But they're just shuttle pilots, cadets."

"By definition, they're warriors. And warriors,
the moment they sign up, know they may have to
sacrifice their lives."

Apollo shouted at his father's back:

"Sacrifice, yes, but not throw them away!"

Adama turned back to face his son.

"What do you estimate your losses would be?"

"One Cylon attack and—and I could lose the
entire squadron."

They stared at each other angrily, then Adama
spoke in a gentler voice:

"You could leave the, uh, the lesser qualified
pilots behind."

Is that what he's thinking, Apollo wondered, *that
I'm registering this protest just to protect Serina? I
want to protect her, yes—desperately—but I
couldn't give her special treatment. Like he said, she
signed on as a warrior. Still . . . it must be hard for
him to make the concession. But, no, I can't allow it.*

"I appreciate what you're saying, father. But in
my opinion *none* of the pilots are qualified to fly this
mission. If I hold one of them back, I have to hold
them all back. That's it. You must reconsider. I can't
agree to this mission."

"Your disagreement is theoretical, I presume. If
ordered to fly it, you will."

The words were spoken in the clipped, precise
way that Adama used to convey the strength of his

will. They were the challenge, the gauntlet thrown to test the outspoken subordinate.

"Of course I'll fly it. If so ordered."

"Thank you. Your protest will be logged accordingly. Prepare your squadron."

"Yes, sir."

Apollo resisted the compelling urge to continue the argument. The autocratic coolness in his father's eyes made it clear that the discussion was closed.

Cassiopeia's gaze had been fixed on the monitoring console for so long that she was beginning to feel more like a photographic device than a human being. Each of the medical analytic units that were scanning the patients recorded similar data. The overall message of this tour of duty was, no change. All lights blinked yellow; no reds had started flashing in some time. Doctor Salik had commented that perhaps the spread of the disease had been stabilized. No new cases had been reported in several duty-tours, after all. She almost wanted one of the patients in the cryo-tubes to go critical, so she could press a button, raise a temperature level, increase an intraven-feed, just to be doing something.

She sensed a movement behind her. Looking around, she saw Captain Apollo, his face paled by the yellow light shooting upward from Lieutenant Boomer's cryo-tube. He peered down at Boomer sadly. Glad to get a break from watching the console, she walked to him. He seemed oblivious to her approach.

"Anything I can do for you, Captain?"

Close up, Apollo's face seemed ashen, and not just because of the color-draining yellow light.

"Any new word on his chances?" he asked.

It was the same question he asked every time he

stopped by life station, and he stopped by at least twice a day. She had to give him the same answer.

"Not good. Unless we can find the cause of the infection."

He looked at her, his eyes still sad.

"Well," he said, "I guess we're going to try to do something about that."

"I know. I hope that—"

"Don't say it, Cassie. Just don't say it."

He looked down at Boomer again. Involuntarily his hand reached out and touched the surface of the cold tube, stroked it as if he had accepted it as a substitute for Boomer's forehead.

Studying the captain's strained, unhappy face, Cassiopeia wanted to take the man into her arms and comfort him. Each time she saw how deeply compassion ran in Apollo, she wished a man like him could come into her life. Not Apollo, but a man like him—Apollo, after all, was in love with Serina, a woman who certainly did deserve him. Cassiopeia seemed continually to run up against and become involved with the game players, the cheerful and charming womanizers like Starbuck who, she must admit, were great fun. However, when it came to any expression of love from such a man, forget it. Starbuck'd rather hang onto the tail-end of a viper in flight than stick to a woman steadily. That was her luck, and sometimes it pained her to think of it.

Apollo interrupted her bitter reveries by saying:

"We all appreciate what you're doing, Cassiopeia."

She laughed. She had not intended to laugh, but she did.

"I don't do anything. I sit and watch, flip a lever, press a button."

"That's something like we all do."

"Yeah, I guess. But somehow it comes out

different when you do it than when I do it."

"Well, I have to go muster a squadron. Just keep taking care of these guys and we'll see if we can bring you back a cure."

"I regard that as a promise, Captain."

Inside Boomer the organism that had invaded him was quiescent, numbed by the cold which the cryo-tube maintained at a steady level. Eventually it could adjust to the cold and revive, but for now it was held in suspension just like its host. Its revival would mean the end of its own existence as well as its host's. Fortunately, it was not hampered by fears of mortality, so it could not perceive its own impending doom—that, when Boomer died, it would die, too.

Gemi could hardly keep her eyes open. Every time she concentrated on the print of the book she was holding—*Ancient Virgon Ethical Systems: The Other Side of Self-Absorption*—it seemed to blur into dials, gauges, scanner images, and readouts, perhaps because all those items were forever imprinted on her brain from staring at them so long and so hard during the intensive training sessions, or from her one and only solo flight, which had amounted to no more than a joyride around the awesomely beautiful outside of the *Galactica*. She might never be able to read again.

Looking around the room, a dining area converted into a leisure space for cadets, she noticed a distinct lethargy in all her fellow cadets. Dietra sat with her paintbrush resting on her palette, looking for all the world as if she did not intend to put another stroke onto her half-finished painting of a still-life setup. Carrie was laconically trying to show Brie her collection of spice containers, with examples of the art from all the twelve worlds, but neither Carrie nor Brie seemed interested in the intricate variety of containers displayed unmethodically on the table in front of them. Everyone was just plain tired out from all the work they'd put in since classes had begun.

Gemi finally capitulated to her tiredness and closed her eyes. Immediately images of training began swimming on her inner eyelids. She drifted into a dream about her mock-viper—she was like a child, lost in its Piscean-leather seat, her short arms not quite able to reach the controls, her feet just dangling over the seat edge. Battle raged all around her. A Cylon ship was making a run toward her. Scrambling across the seat, which seemed to be growing in size, she reached out from it to the joystick. With an excruciating effort, she managed to draw the stick to her and press its firing button. She watched the Cylon ship explode in slow motion, pieces of it passing her ship like driftwood. Suddenly Starbuck was beside her in the compartment, patting her head in approval—treating her like the dream-child she was, but at least giving her attention. (Here she was third in the class, behind Serina and Dietra, and he still rarely even gave her a criticism, much less a compliment.) "I'm really a woman, you know," she said to the smiling condescending lieutenant. "A full-bodied one, though I may not look like—"

She was shaken out of her dream by Dietra.

"C'mon child," Dietra was saying.

"C'mon what? What's—"

"Action, baby. We are assigned duty."

"But that's im—"

"I know, I know. Don't rock the boat, especially not a boat the size of the *Galactica*. We're going to fly an escort mission. You're my wingmate, darling. So wake up and fly right, okay?"

Gemi shook the last vestiges of sleep off and ran after Dietra. Among the thoughts that raced through her mind was the vow that now was the chance to impress Starbuck. Skill in battle would have to turn his head.

Briefly, she wondered if maneuvering a viper across space would be as easy as manipulating a mockflight viper in test chamber or soloing around a battlestar.

As if held near the screen by an eerie occult force, Adama hovered by the launch control station, looking over Rigel's shoulder at the humming, buzzing, and flickering devices. Rigel, intent on studying every aspect of the launch, seemed unaware of her commander's presence.

Adama observed that neither Starbuck nor Apollo looked too happy as they approached their fighters. They both disapproved of this mission, he knew. Perhaps any combat-hardened veteran would. Adama realized that it might be folly to send out a contingent of inexperienced pilots, but there were times when such risks were necessary. As Salik had pointed out at briefing, either way we chance losing a squadron, whether the tyro pilots in their unfamiliar vipers or the afflicted ones back in sick bay.

"Medical shuttle taking off from Flight Deck One," Rigel said. "Will rendezvous with Blue Squadron at coordinates Alpha three seven."

The shuttle's takeoff was reasonably smooth, considering that it was piloted by one of the least qualified of trainees. Tension on the bridge heightened as everyone awaited the signal to launch for the new cadets, knowing that anything could go wrong on a launch, especially when most of the pilots were so inexperienced.

Rigel took a deep breath, received the signal to launch from Tigh, and announced:

"Transferring control to viper fighters. Launch when ready."

Members of the crew not vitally concerned with duties concerning mission launch gathered anxiously around monitor screens. Starbuck's voice came over the main commline:

"Remember, just like we did it on the simulators and in the individual solo flights. And don't forget how sensitive these controls are, ladies."

A couple of grumbles on the commline forced him to append:

"Ah, sorry."

"Blue Squadron," said Apollo. "Let's show the fleet how the launch is done. Blue Squadron Leader, launching."

Apollo's viper rocketed down the launch bay tube and out. The precision and skill of his action seemed to lend spirit to the rest of the squadron. One by one they blasted into space with the efficiency of veterans, although the subsequent formation was a bit shaky and uneven. Starbuck provided a running commentary on their difficulties:

"Easy, Dietra, steady. Easy. You're coming up too fast. You should—that's better. Good job. Serina, watch your spacing. Stick tight to your leaders, all of you."

The last cadet's viper zoomed out of launch tube and suddenly seemed to lose control, go into a spin.

"Brie!" Starbuck's voice was tense but steady. "Take back control. Back on the power, back on the power. Get your autocontrol—that's good. You've got it. You're steady. You did it, Brie! You did it!"

Rigel turned away from her monitor and smiled.

"Blue Squadron launched," she hollered, and

several members of the bridge crew worked up a weary but enthusiastic cheer.

"Blue Squadron leader to *Galactica*," Apollo radioed. "We're on our way!"

Adama gave a great sigh of relief and retreated from launch control station. He almost backed right into Tigh, who had obviously been hovering near with the same watchful anxiety as his commander.

"Come to my quarters with me, Colonel," Adama said. "We'll talk there."

Tigh followed silently. Both men said nothing until they had passed through the entranceway to the commander's compartment.

"Our course?" Adama asked.

"We're dead on course, sir. It will not be long until we have reached the outer perimeter of the void."

Adama nodded, then stared into Tigh's eyes and said:

"You disapprove of my leading the fleet into the void."

"It's not my place to—"

"Stop that, Tigh. Come down off your epaulets. I need someone to talk to."

Both men sat. Tigh looked more relaxed the next time he spoke:

"Adama, for all we know that void could be endless. And we *do* know from scanner readouts pulled from Apollo's and Starbuck's ships that it's so magnetically charged that we almost lost both men out there. Once we move beyond any visual contact with the stars and can't plot course, we can wind up lost, tied up in that dense black maelstrom forever. Sorry to say this, Commander, but I think I'd rather take my chances against Cylon attack."

Now that he had gotten all that off his chest, Tigh

settled back into his chair. Adama cocked his head quizzically and asked:

"What if we *had* a reference point to guide on in the void?"

Tigh shrugged. "But there is none."

From the surface of his desk, Adama picked up a tattered and yellowed book.

"This volume, the Koboliana, sometimes called the Book of the Word, tells us of a great star that guided the people of Kobol from their withered and desiccated planet across what is described here as an endless black sea."

Tigh leaned forward.

"This endless sea, you're saying it's the void?"

"It could be. I think it is."

Tigh sat back again, looking puzzled.

"Commander, I'd—I'd like to be sustained by such faith as yours. You know I've never been able to—to make my peace with the doctrine in that book. I'd like to believe that the twelve worlds originated on some forgotten planet somewhere, and that its peoples found it necessary to flee as their sun died and their homelands dried up. But, I'm sorry, to me it's all legend, myth. The kind of supportive values that make up a religion. I'm sorry, I really am. I feel a heretic's pain whenever this subject comes up."

Adama continued to stare at his aide, who felt that the power of his commander's eyes might just be as bright as the legendary star he had referred to.

"Adama," Tigh continued, "even if I accept your idea of the mythic void and the bright, beaconlike star, there are, well, there're probably as many voids in the universe as doubtful ideas. Who's to say if this is the same one? And even if it was, how can we be sure that your interpretation of the data—and that of the Koboliana, for that matter—is at all accurate? Our ancestors tended to view all events as manifestations of deities rather than science."

"You don't believe it really happened?"

"I merely think that what appeared as a great guiding light might have been some kind of astronomical phenomenon not at all connected with the beliefs that have been attributed to it. Perhaps it was not a beacon of faith but merely a fortunate star or sun that they followed because a discovery of science indicated they should. Forgive me, Adama, I am just not a believer, you know that."

Adama thought over Tigh's comments for a moment, then he opened a drawer of his desk and took out a box. Raising the lid of the box delicately, as if its contents might be radioactive, he removed a breastplate, a roughly circular piece of dark blue stone encased in a gold-tinted metal setting.

"Old friend," Adama said, "this breastplate contains a stone which legend says was carried from the home planet Kobol. I may wear it as a member of the council, but it is also the symbol of our faith, representing the old Lords of Kobol and their beliefs. I must respond to it, must follow where its spirit impels me."

"Its . . . its *spirit*?"

"Yes, Tigh." Adama's voice had grown more impassioned. "I can feel its powers even as I hold it. I cannot deny it, turn my back on the inspiration which delivered our people once before. Why do you look at me like that?"

"It just occurred to me that you might be crazy."

Adama laughed. A quite sane-sounding laugh, as it happened.

"No, I'm not crazy. But men moved by such overwhelming forces usually appear crazy to the people around them, I'm told."

"So do people who are just plain crazy when they talk about . . . about *forces* that don't exist. With all due respect, sir—"

"We will enter the void."

"I realize that. I only hope that you're right."

"Trust me."

"I always do. And it always works out. It's just that the time it doesn't work out may be the end of everything."

"I understand that as well as you. But we must take the risk."

"Yes, sir."

The relaxed tone of a talk between friends had gone out of Tigh's voice. He was all duty now. Adama wished they could have stayed calm and intimate, discussing the volatile subject in an abstract, gentlemanly fashion, but there were times when it was best to restore the sense of *Galactica*'s hierarchy. After Tigh had saluted and left, Adama stayed behind, staring at the breastplate as if it might suddenly reveal its truth to him.

CHAPTER EIGHT

SERINA: Serina here. I don't know where to begin this time. I don't even know what I feel. Or should feel. I've had my first taste of battle. The hard part, the part I don't know how to deal with, is that—for a short while at least—I liked it. I blasted a Cylon raider out of the skies. Just like a hotshot pilot. And I liked it. I felt a sense of elation. I was happy when I got back to the *Galactica*. Serina, flying ace. The Joystick Cutie of Blue Squadron. All of us were hysterically happy. In the ready-room we babbled about our maneuvers, our kills, as if they were matters of gossip at a tea party. Myself included. I led the chorus. Now I'm not so sure I feel good about it at all.

I'm a warrior, I guess.

So much for lingering doubts and troubled

reflections, on with the report. We headed straight for the asteroid where Boomer and Jolly had detected the Cylon outpost. Apollo, as flight commander, led the way. As soon as he had the asteroid on-scanner, he tightened the formation, holding the escort squadron out of possible Cylon artillery range. Then he announced he would attempt a low-level approach from a different angle, to catch the Cylons by surprise before they could scramble fighters.

"If I get lucky," he said, "we won't have to risk the squadron."

My heart was in my throat, I was so afraid for him. All I could think of was why did we have to risk so much? My thoughts then strayed to more selfish levels. Cynically, I wondered if it was right for our life together to depend on the insignificant, rocky, hideous asteroid below us. I realized how important the research mission was, but I was angry that Apollo was planning such an enormous risk.

Dietra, the cadet who's displayed the most talent for leadership, questioned Apollo's decision, saying that our best shot at surprising the Cylons was to all go down there together. She told me later that she thought Apollo, Starbuck, and our other instructors were mollycoddling us and she resented that. We deserved our chance to prove ourselves; we were capable of handling it. Apollo suggested that Dietra demonstrate her abilities by following orders, then he went in. His viper seemed to diminish in size to a tiny dot as it descended toward the asteroid. I don't think I ever felt so frightened in my life. For a moment I was certain that I wouldn't see him again.

I didn't have much time for such self-indulgent emotions, because Brie broke commline silence by informing Starbuck that she was picking up a blip on her scanner in a rear quadrant. At first he made

light of her observation. Brie, after all, had
exhibited a strong slant toward emotional thinking
and action all during training. Starbuck thought she
had just, in her overeager way, mistaken the medical
shuttle for some other craft, and he told her so.
There was a long silence, during which I thought I
heard Brie make a couple of stuttering starts toward
another communication. Finally, in a terribly meek
voice, she said she didn't think it was the shuttle and,
not only that, it was closing in on us. Starbuck, still
believing it was the medical ship, angrily shouted
that he'd ordered Salik's crew to hold position.
Finally, he analyzed the image on his own scanner
and realized that the tiny blip inside one of its
squares could not be the shuttle, after all. Brie had
been right. (I must admit I felt a small sense of
triumph for the cadet class.)

Starbuck cursed and flew off to engage the
intruder. Athena pulled her ship out of formation
and followed him. She told me later that, when she'd
drawn up even with him, he had been quite irritated.
He asked her what she thought she was doing and
started to read her out royally. Well, that got
Athena's back up but she kept cool anyway. She
informed him that she was, after all, his wingman,
and wingmen were supposed to protect each other.
He muttered something, and told her to stay out of
his way. That really got her, she said, and she started
repeating to herself, "Keep it up, Starbuck, just keep
it up." She was somewhat soothed by the chantlike
aspect of the utterance.

Then the Cylon raider zoomed into physical
view. As Athena tells it, she and Starbuck
immediately forgot their differences and acted in
concert like the well-trained team they were. Athena
went highside, while Starbuck dropped to the low

position. The Cylon ship, used to this kind of trap, changed course and made to slip away from the double-pronged assault. Both Athena and Starbuck had anticipated the enemy move. They knew the Cylon crew would maneuver into a position where it could return fire, while Athena and Starbuck worked their controls adjusting to the shift. Catching the Cylon fighter with simultaneous bursts of fire, they watched it explode. Since they were aware that the Cylon crew had had time to warn the outpost, Starbuck and Athena had no time to admire their victory. They headed back toward the asteroid and the squadron.

At the same time Starbuck was informing us of impending danger from the outpost, Apollo was just setting his viper into its low-level approach on the enemy stronghold. Before we could warn him off, the rock-wall camouflage of the Cylon base pulled away and raiders started roaring out. Apollo said later it looked like bursts of fire suddenly erupting from the surface of the asteroid. The lead ship flew in his direction but obviously did not suspect the presence of a vanguard that close to base. Apollo was able to get the enemy ship in his sights and fire. The disintegration of the Cylon craft alerted the next one in line and it turned toward Apollo. The advantage of surprise still with him, Apollo destroyed that ship, too. As he whipped up and over the hole in the rock wall that was the Cylon launch site, he briefly feasted his eyes on an entire squadron of Cylon raiders, all moving toward the opening.

I can still hear his voice coming over the commline:

"Blue Squadron. Apollo. They're launching. The sky here is about to be full of enemy ships. Return to

Galactica! Repeat, return to *Galactica*!"

Dietra said, "Ignore the order. We can't leave Apollo behind. No way!"

She pointed her ship downward. A moment later, the rest of us hotshots followed suit. My feelings at that moment were definitely mixed. I wanted to be down there helping Apollo, desperately, but I was scared stiff for myself. Fortunately, in battle situations one has little time to consider the psychological limits or philosophical ramifications of such a problem. The next thing I knew, I was part of a phalanx of ships zeroing in on another phalanx of ships.

"I ordered all of you back," Apollo yelled.

"After this run, Captain," Dietra said. She sounded as if she were smiling.

I didn't have much time or opportunity to monitor the actions of my fellow warriors in the aerial combat, for a Cylon fighter was heading right at me immediately. Fortunately, I automatically clicked into battle mode and my thumb moved quickly and instinctively to the middle button on my joystick, the one governing my laser weapon. One blast, one simple blast, and that Cylon ship became fragments of metal flying in all directions, some right at my cockpit, it seemed. For a moment, I thought of the spark of life that I took away from the three Cylon pilots, and I hated myself for turning killer, no matter how justifiable the cause. I wasn't able to contemplate this particular moral dilemma at length, however, for there was another Cylon ship nestling into my sights. I got it, too, split it into its prime components with one steady on-target shot. The second killing was easier. I felt happy. I had proven myself. All those doubts about me and the other cadets being qualified to fly vipers were fading fast. I had little time to enjoy my elation because another Cylon ship was sweeping toward me. It should have knocked me right out of the skies, but Brie had seen it first and she hit it just before it would have destroyed me. Later, I could not stop thanking Brie.

As I was busy qualifying for fighter-stripes on my flight helmet, Apollo had recovered from his surprise at our arrival on the scene and had formulated his plan. Streaking toward the Cylon post, he shouted for us to stay on the enemy craft while he went for their launch bay. Opening fire on the hole itself, he first disintegrated a new pair of Cylon raiders about to launch. Then he flew dangerously close to the hole, firing wildly. His shots hit something. As he pulled out of the dive, fire and exploding fragments suddenly erupted outward from the Cylon base.

The rest was just a wipe-up operation. All of us came through with flying colors, shooting down most of the remaining Cylon fighters. We missed only a trio of ships, that swept away from us and out into space, evidently to carry the news of our whereabouts to another Cylon post or base ship.

As Apollo realigned with our formation, Dietra congratulated him for his splendid shooting, and I was pleased by his gracious response. None of the Starbuckian brashness for my husband-to-be. He called my name, and I acknowledged: "Right here, Apollo," and he seemed relieved to hear my voice. He then congratulated the squadron on a job well done.

Well, the report's not in yet on what the medical team found on that desolate asteroid. They're doing tests right now, and I'll dutifully record their findings later.

After we got back here, we all seemed to feel the need for release and we gathered in the *Galactica*'s officers' club. Drinking, singing, and generally raising hell like seasoned veterans. Dietra kept talking of the number of Cylon ships she'd destroyed personally. Brie was amazed she'd functioned at all. Carrie could not get off the subject of how well she'd maneuvered her ship. Gemi, her small, chunky body looking taller and stronger, kept asking us if she had performed all right, and we kept telling her that destroying three enemy craft, as she had done, was at the very least an adequate display of her warrior skills.

When Apollo and Starbuck joined us, I think they felt left out. Here we were, green cadets, bragging about our conquests—and there they were, two pilots who'd been through more battles than there are dents on a transport ship, discussing the preparations for the wedding between Apollo and myself. As he mentioned the bargain he'd received in trading for a pair of curtains with a weaver aboard the colonial mover's freighter, he sent me an overtheatrical wink. I sobered up a bit from my combat binge. Before the disease struck the *Galactica*'s squadrons, my thoughts had centered on my love for Apollo and the wedding. Now I was so concerned about what a cracking good pilot I'd become that I'd forgotten all that, momentarily at least. I went into a temporary funk, stirring out of it only when I realized how Brie was telling me in great detail how, even with the G-suit, her vision had grayed at the edges in one sweep. And Sorrel was going on about how the real attack was nothing like what we'd experienced in the simulators.

Suddenly I knew I had to get away. I felt so sad. I returned here and started recording. I feel better now. Not good, but better.

CHAPTER NINE

Lucifer glided along a corridor to the base-star command chamber, moving much more quickly than usual. He was unusually eager to view Baltar's reaction to the news he brought. The human had been so sure of himself, it would be intriguing to see how he would respond to a major setback. Lucifer's interest was quite academic. He had been studying Baltar for so long now, the man had become his special project, one whose reactions must be observed and recorded.

Lucifer entered the command room at such a high speed, he almost forgot to decelerate. He might have collided with the base of the pedestal if he had not transmitted through his ambulatory circuits the message to apply the brakes to the treads at the bottom of his nether limbs.

"By your command," he said, as soon as he had come to a stop. His bow toward the pedestal was abrupt and hardly sincere. His obsequious overlay personality seemed to be decaying rapidly. He would have to see that he monitored himself much more severely in the future.

"Speak," Baltar said, his diction so precise it seemed to be providing its own echo.

"Vipers from the *Galactica* have attacked and destroyed our outpost."

There was no response from the human. Instead, he mulled over Lucifer's report before speaking again:

"Then the *Galactica* is on her way over the outpost now!"

"No."

Baltar's bushy eyebrows raised.

"No?" he said.

"She is entering the void."

Baltar sank back into his throne, his eyes darting around, as if trying to find an answer printed somewhere on the blue-gray metal walls of the command chamber.

"Is something troubling you, sir?"

"Yes. Why do they bother risking detection by destroying the outpost if it was not to be part of their route, if they had no intention of moving in that direction? It makes no sense. Unless perhaps..."

"Perhaps what, Baltar?"

"Adama must have needed something from that asteroid. Food? Fuel?"

"Anyone searching for food or fuel on that particular asteroid would be disappointed."

Baltar gripped the arms of his throne tightly.

"We will have to consider that question further. Is there anything more to report, Lucifer?"

"Well, there is one other curious matter, one I

don't quite know how to compute."

"Out with it! What?"

"It seems that the colonial vipercraft reportedly flew in other than their normal fashion."

"Other than normal? What do you mean?"

"At times they did not seem in complete control of such elementals as formation and aerial maneuver."

"Evidently they flew well enough to destroy your base."

"It was a small outpost. Caught by surprise, since you determined the *Galactica* would not strike there."

Baltar smiled sinisterly.

"Do not fence with me, my friend." The way he said *my friend* did not, to Lucifer, indicate any genuine comradeship. "Everything is still proceeding well enough. What of your part? You have not captured one of their pilots as I ordered."

Lucifer, expecting the question, had his answer ready.

"To assure such a capture, we would have to risk being discovered. Therefore, the order contradicts an earlier one, that we keep our ships out of the *Galactica*'s scanner range."

Baltar's eyes widened in anger.

"They send out patrols, do they not? Capture one."

Lucifer glided out of the command chamber, wondering just how he could fulfill one of Baltar's orders without jeopardizing another. Craftily, he suspected.

The excited clamor of voices in the *Galactica* officers' club sounded like the raucous din of an off-limits cabaret. Gemi, in the rare times when she said anything, could not hear herself speak. Ever since they had returned from battle, the trainees could not stop talking about their own individual achievements. They seemed intent on turning the episode into fleet legend *immediately*.

"I popped the first one rising up," Dietra was saying, "then did an alpha turn and came back in on a second."

"That's when I did a half-roll and my second volley blew his outer tip off," Carrie interjected, her boast overlapping Dietra's.

Serina joined the chorus:

"It all happened so fast, I forgot about deflection and hyper boosters, I just kept firing."

Gemi wondered why she could not participate in the fugue of joy and braggadocio. She must look pretty silly, sitting here quietly and listening to the others rhapsodize about their flying skills and kills. Gemi had flown well, Serina had told her that, but nevertheless she felt disoriented, and more than a little disappointed. Every nerve in her body seemed to have divided like an amoeba, just to make her doubly jittery. The battle, for her, had been essentially no different from a simulator session. All she really cared about now was whether she had done well, whether her grades were good or not.

Starbuck and Apollo joined the group and appeared to derive some amusement out of the noisy battle chatter. Gemi kept sneaking looks at Starbuck, hoping he would smile over at her and say she'd done well. She needed no more attention from him right now than that. But his glance kept sweeping casually past her, and he addressed specific remarks only to the others. She felt lost in the oversized chair and wondered if she should stand on its seat to attract attention. Once Apollo grinned her way and reached over to pat the back of her hand. Starbuck didn't even notice the captain's action.

Looking at her fellow warriors as they gabbed away joyfully, she began to hate feeling like an outsider. Who were they anyway, these hotshot skypilots? People who were sculptured beautifully, who could talk smoothly, who could move like graceful jungle animals? She often wondered what it would be like to go inside them and feel things the way they felt them. Could they go inside her, understand and perceive the way she felt? Perhaps they could not. They knew what it was like to be attractive, top of the heap, skilled beyond normal expectations. It was conceivable that they could not begin to understand someone who did not have these traits. Maybe the gleaming facets of their lives were so well defined that they could not understand lives that begged such definition. She wondered if she should envy them for the clarity of their existences or condemn them for not being able to perceive entities who lived in darkness. She should probably not do either. She should probably drink her drink and try to create some joyful banter of her own. If she could not really be one of them, she could be a copy of one of them.

Why didn't Starbuck ever look her way?

"I was confused, you know?" Brie was saying. "There were vipers and Cylons everywhere. I was afraid to fire my lasers for fear of hitting one of you. Then this Cylon passed me inverted. Doing a high drop toward the surface. Before I knew it I was on his tail...and zap!"

"Zap," Gemi muttered.

"What was that, Gemi?" Dietra asked.

"Oh, nothing."

"Speak up, child. You're a part of the team, you know."

"Yes, I know."

"Don't be shy about it. Bellow it out!"

"YES, I KNOW!"

"That's more like it, baby."
And it was.

The organism inside Boomer had no awareness of its own decline. It did not even feel weak as the numbing substance injected into the host's body infiltrated the outer membranelike layers of the organism. It merely became numb, weakened, then lost all awareness as it died, its last moment having no more significance than any other of its living moments.

It was a long time after the cold gases had been withdrawn before Boomer became aware of the fact that he had been stored in a cryo-tube. Even Cassiopeia's softly whispered explanations of his disease and its treatment did not really get through to his brain the first times they were spoken. The story of Dr. Salik's detection of the organism's existence on the asteroid, of his quick, frantic researches into its characteristics, and of the almost accidental discovery that it could be destroyed by a simple potassium-based compound, all seemed to Boomer a disconnected dream. The only part he really responded to was the description of how Apollo, Starbuck, and a contingent of inexperienced cadets had performed the lifesaving flight. When he passed out again, it was to dream of those adventurers. He watched Starbuck, his sly, impish glance darting everywhere, lead a part of the squadron. Then his dream became confused as Starbuck's voice intruded upon it.

"Boomer? . . . Boomer, can you hear me?"

He awakened suddenly and opened his eyes. There, standing above him—his form partially distorted by the leftover moisture from the cryogenic process that was still graying the window—was Starbuck, looking quite concerned and happy at the same time. Behind him stood Apollo, his face showing similar sympathy.

"How do you feel, buddy?" Starbuck asked.

It took a long while for Boomer's brain to make the synaptical connections that allowed him to discern any feeling at all in his body. Inside, he felt drained, hollow, as if there might be nothing left there.

"I heard what you did, fellas. You...and the others...Thanks..."

Starbuck and Apollo exchanged a smiling glance, then the captain said:

"How do you feel?"

He couldn't keep his eyes open as dizziness seemed to come over him in a wave.

"Awful. I feel awful. But it beats being dead."

He squeezed his eyes tight and slipped back to sleep.

After the return of the squadron, with its heartening report that the mission had been successful, Tigh confronted Adama with his last impassioned plea to reconsider the command decision to enter the void. Adama listened patiently, then reminded his aide that the survivors of the Cylon outpost battle would alert every nearby enemy base.

"At least the void will offer us some cover," he pointed out.

"If there are any of us left to find," Tigh responded angrily.

Adama glared at the colonel, then said softly:

"We're going in."

However, once inside the void, with its blackness surrounding them, even Adama began to have some doubts. He sent out a general order that the fleet maintain a tight formation. In spite of this directive, distress signals kept coming in from the commercial and transport vehicles whose panicked skippers were encountering difficulty maintaining their fix on the battlestar.

"Navigation reports instruments fluctuating rapidly from magnetic interference," Omega said, his voice shaky as he tried to hold in his fear.

Everybody, it seemed, was spooked by the occult suggestions of the void. There was a definite feeling of impending doom even among the sensible members of the *Galactica*'s crew. Tigh couldn't get the worried look off his face and the usually impassive Rigel, a woman of few words outside her job, had become chatty and nervous. Whenever one of them requested a further verification of orders, Adama merely replied quietly that they would stay steady on course.

Tigh gestured Adama to a scanner, saying:

"Commander, could you look at this?"

Adama joined him at the console.

"What is it?" he asked. The screen was blank. Tigh looked puzzled.

"I'm not sure," he said. "It was there, behind us, then it was gone."

Had the eerie aspects of the void affected Tigh's powers of observation?, Adama wondered. Was he driving Tigh and, for that matter, the entire crew too hard, forcing them to do his bidding without the kind of explanations that would at least give them hope?

"Field looks clear to me," Adama said gently.

"Now it does, but every once in a while—there, look."

A small, fuzzy outline that might have been anything drifted in from the right side of the screen, then disappeared abruptly.

"Meteorite track?" Adama asked Tigh.

"Doubt it. It's always in the same quadrants. Delta nine. If it's a meteorite, it's following us. I think it's Cylons."

Adama stared at the screen for a long while before replying. During that time the object appeared and disappeared one more time.

"It may be," he finally said. "There's only one way to find out. Assemble a patrol."

As Tigh followed orders, Adama stood at an observation portal, trying to perceive something in the overwhelming blackness.

CHAPTER TEN

SERINA: I can't work myself out of this peculiar mood. I don't know what to feel. Here Apollo and I are finally getting married and yet it's so spoiled because we don't know what's happened to Starbuck. Apollo believes he's dead.

Maybe I better report all this chronologically. It's strange to believe it all happened over such a short period of time.

Yesterday, before going to the officers' club, I checked the duty roster and saw that Apollo and I were both on patrol alert. In the new roster I had been designated his wingman. For obvious reasons I was quite happy about it.

At the club, it seemed everybody was still on the subject of the mission and all the brilliant maneuvers we pulled off above that Cylon asteroid. Dietra and Brie, especially, were holding forth enthusiastically. Just after I arrived, Apollo came in. He didn't notice me and joined Starbuck at the bar. I excused myself from the others and started walking toward them. At that moment Colonel Tigh came running into the room and up to Apollo and Starbuck. Although I didn't hear what he said at the time, I found out later that he was ordering them to launch bay. They were just leaving the bar when I caught Apollo's attention and asked him where he was going. He said there was just a routine matter that the three of them had to attend to. I felt definitely left out, and angry about it, so I followed them out to the corridor.

I asked what was up and Tigh, with a cautious look toward Apollo, said:

"I'm afraid this is confidential. It's a mission."

Ah-ha, I thought, my turn to strike a blow for the cadet corps. I said to Tigh:

"You've got the wrong pilot here in Starbuck for any mission. According to duty roster, I'm Apollo's wingman. If Apollo goes, I go!"

Tigh looked surprised that anyone would question anything he did, while Apollo acted quite angry. I pointed out that the orders were posted and must be followed. Tigh reluctantly agreed and Starbuck said it was fine by him, he'd rather spend the time back at the bar. If only he had returned to the club, he'd still be around. If I'd replaced him properly, perhaps all of us would have survived the incident. Or I'd be dead instead.

Anyway, Starbuck briskly trod off down the corridor, shouting back to us over his shoulder that we should have a nice, peaceful mission. As we accompanied Tigh to launch bay, he explained that scanners had picked up a possible pursuit force and that our mission was to verify its existence.

As we waited for the elevator to launch bay, I was disturbed by the bizarre behavior of Starbuck. I commented to Apollo that we might have hurt Starbuck's feelings. Apollo said he doubted that, since Starbuck hadn't gone back to the officers' club. I didn't get his drift—that Starbuck must be up to something typically devious—until we arrived at launch bay and saw him in full gear climbing into his viper. Apollo did not appear too surprised to see him.

Tigh shouted at Starbuck that he was violating orders, but Starbuck just smiled back and gave the signal to launch. His power had engaged before Tigh could order him off the mission.

"What's he doing?" I asked Apollo, who replied that he was trying to protect one of us, or both. Apollo then kissed me quickly and ran toward his own viper. I tried to run after him, but Tigh grabbed my shoulders and held me back.

"Wait a minute," I cried out, "I'm his wingman."

Tigh told me to let them go, but I squirmed out of his grasp, raced to my ship and virtually leaped into its cockpit. I had all systems rumbling and ready to go in no time at all. I gave the signal to launch without looking back at Tigh who, I'm sure, must have been furious over the many acts of insubordination that he had witnessed in such a short time. The launch crew had no idea what was happening, but they activated the release and my viper went hurtling down the launch tube and out of the *Galactica*.

I'm told there was considerable confusion on the bridge when it was realized that the normal two-ship scout patrol had been enlarged by one.

I listened to Apollo and Starbuck over the commline as I caught up with them. Starbuck was going too fast, and Apollo cautioned him not to get too far ahead or he'd lose his fix. In the void, of course, that would have been a proper disaster. Starbuck eased up and let Apollo follow him more closely.

As I reached Apollo's position, I thought it'd be exactly what he deserved if I pulled alongside him to officially announce, as it were, my presence. He was positively snappish when he realized there was a third ship and it was mine.

"Serina," he shouted, "you get your tail back aboard the *Galactica*."

I asked him, in as cool a voice as I could, was that any way to talk to an officer, and I threatened to have him up on charges as soon as we returned.

"Or, at the very least," I added, "lock you out of my chambers."

He said he had faith in my piloting abilities, such as they were (I resisted commenting on that), but that they didn't apply to the void.

"The void can swallow up good pilots. So go back."

Starbuck interrupted our little domestic spat with the news that whatever it was the *Galactica* had picked up on her scanners, it was still beyond our range. He couldn't go any farther without losing his fix on the *Galactica*. He suggested that Apollo maintain the home-base fix while he kept a fix on Apollo, thereby doubling the range. I saw my opening and rushed in. (Again, perhaps if I'd stayed out of it, Starbuck would still be with us, but . . .) I proposed that Apollo could lock on me while I maintained the *Galactica* fix, thereby *tripling* our range. Starbuck was so surprised to hear my voice, he almost couldn't follow the logic. He and Apollo had a little colloquy about who had the right to go forward, with Apollo arguing that as flight commander he should go on deep probe. Starbuck, however, had the dialectical advantage, since he was already out there. He zoomed ahead, telling us to consider his move as our first wedding present. (I suppose that now, if he could communicate with us, he'd say it was a genuine wedding present, since he saved our lives by giving up his own. Oh, Starbuck . . .)

What light his boosters cast back to us across the void dissipated quickly. Apollo and I were left alone, with only the dim lights from our helmet rims and from the control panel to provide any illumination within the void's intense darkness. I reported back to the *Galactica* what we were attempting. Tigh, his voice still displaying a shade of anger at the precipitous actions of his trio of brazenly cavalier pilots, approved our plan. I told Apollo, who tried to communicate with Starbuck. Starbuck's voice came back too faintly and Apollo ordered him to diminish speed. We don't know if he followed that order or not. The next thing we knew he was shouting:

"Targets!"

Apollo requested further transmission, telling Starbuck to pull back and wait for him before engaging targets. Starbuck apparently didn't hear, for he said that he was practically on top of them. Then, suddenly:

"I *am* on top of them!"

There was a long, staticky silence, then his next communication:

"Apollo, I'm in trouble!"

Apollo asked what was happening but the response began to break up into sound fragments. I heard Starbuck shout Apollo's name and the word, "Communicate." Apollo repeatedly tried to get through to him. His last communication was the word, "Cylons."

Apollo and I, hemmed in by the limitations of our double fix on the *Galactica*, waited a long while before we knew there would be no more transmissions from him.

Finally Apollo said it was no use, he'd been getting nothing but static and silence for too long now, there was no choice but to return to the *Galactica*. It had all happened so quickly, I couldn't believe there was nothing more to be done. When I tried to protest to Apollo, he merely repeated in a sterner voice that we were heading back to home ship.

We flew back in a silence that seemed longer and darker than the void itself.

Back aboard, our report properly filed, Apollo strode out of his father's quarters without listening to any of the commander's consoling words. He took up position by the scanners, his eyes squinting at their busy but uninformative grids and blips. I stood watch behind him, feeling both his sadness and my own—very, very deeply. We stayed like that for an impossibly long time, then I suddenly couldn't stand it any more. I put my arm around his shoulders and asked how long he would stay by the screen, staring at it. He said he couldn't believe Starbuck was gone. I knew what he meant. The two men had been together for so long, had fought side by side more times than they could count. I'm sure he was seeing the history of their comradeship as images replacing the grids and blips on the scanner screens.

Suddenly I couldn't hold back my thoughts any longer. I said I understood what Apollo was going through and that we must get married immediately.

"Now?" he said, "right in the middle of—"

"In the middle of what?" I said. "A disaster. A void. An endless night. I don't care, I'm too scared to care. Look what happened to Starbuck. Next time around it could happen to you or me or both of us. I don't want to wait for a moment which may never come."

He pulled out of my embrace and walked away from me. Then he turned back and just stared at me, obviously not knowing what to say.

I asked him if he loved me.

I felt the cutting edge of his words as he said:

"Is that what it would take to prove it to you?"

He was wrong, but I understood his doubts. I must have looked selfish to have said that. I went to him and stared into his troubled eyes.

"I just want every moment we may have left," I said. "Before another moment passes, another mission where..."

I could not finish the sentence. There were just too many terrifying ways to finish it.

"I do love you, Serina," he said, and pulled me into his arms. At that moment I felt that—

Apollo, in anger, shut off the recorder and removed the crystal. He sat for a long time holding it, looking at it as if it would continue to transmit Serina's voice even in his hand. He put his other hand up to his face and tried to wipe away the tears that were flooding from his eyes. Then he sat back in the chair for a long time, in silence and darkness.

CHAPTER ELEVEN

Lucifer enjoyed interrogating the captured prisoner. Here, at least, was a human with a sense of humor. Since he had known only the company of Cylons and Baltar, Lucifer had thought humor a rare commodity, found only in advanced computers. What a change the jaunty, energetic Starbuck was from Baltar! Even though the interview provided no valuable new information, it did add to Lucifer's storage of knowledge about the enemy.

Starbuck was quickly taken aback when he learned that his interrogator, the grotesque creature whose flashing lights seemed part of his corporeality, was actually a walking computer.

"You do not have computers?" Lucifer asked. "I had been informed that you did."

"Of course we do. But generally we don't dress them up in red velvet robes and have them walk about on tiny wheels. Those are tiny wheels you ambulate with, aren't they?"

"I suppose you could call them that. I believe your term for the items that give me locomotion is 'ball bearings.'"

"I know a good game we can play with ball bearings. A gambling game—"

"We don't have time for games. I am interested in your computers. You implied that sometimes your computers are capable of locomotion—walking about, as you said."

"In a way. We have a kind of robot. It's not programmed for very much. Janitorial work, repair on the outside of a ship, solium leak sniffing, cargo-loading. Dirty work, mostly."

"How disgusting! I am sorry I asked. I assume then that your full computers are stationary."

"Yep. Linked of course into a network, but we deem it wiser to keep them stationary, yes. Nor do we give them more than rudimentary personalities. A friendly voice and an ability to formulate questions when data fed them is insufficient."

"How crude. And cruel. When we conquer you, I must strike a blow for the rights of your computers."

Lucifer's revolutionary boast amused Starbuck, and he laughed. Starbuck's laughter intrigued Lucifer, since it was so filled with delight, in remarkable contrast to Baltar, whose laughter always was lined with a sneer or infused with a cruel gruffness.

"Tell me one thing," Starbuck said. "Cylons cannot have become so advanced in cybernetic technology that an entire complicated computer setup like you can be contained in a unit of your size."

"In the first place the Cylons, although they build us, are not as advanced in cybernetics as you think. Once I and others like me had been created, we were able to program our own improvements on our basic design. We have gone far beyond anything the Cylons' scientists conceived. In the second place, you are correct, I am not self-contained. I am able to link with a vast computer operation in the nether regions of this base-star. It is, in fact, quite an arduous task to transfer, as you might say, *all* of me from one ship to another, although we recently were able to do just that. In the third place, I do not take kindly to being referred to as a unit."

"Sorry, chum."

A bizarre throbbing sound, low-pitched, reverberated through the interrogation room. To Starbuck it sounded like a psychotically disturbed alert claxon.

"What's that?" he asked.

"A signal from our leader. He is impatient to see you. We will finish our interview later."

As they hurriedly progressed down the corridor to the command chamber, Lucifer wondered what Starbuck would say if Lucifer revealed to him that he carried, in his shoulder, a soul of his own creation.

Starbuck followed his Cylon guards docilely into the command chamber. As the doors eased shut behind them, he rubbed his eyes and took a long look around the vaultlike room. Speaking over his shoulder to Lucifer, he remarked:

"I like the way you haven't gone overboard on furniture."

Lucifer, meshing data from his studies of human life and behavior, recalled that there was indeed a bit more luxury in human furniture. He filed an instruction to review this subject when he was more inclined toward passive contemplation.

Starbuck drew a cigar out of his flight jacket pocket and, with an adept twist of wrist, struck a match on the chest plate of the nearest centurion. When the match burst into flame, he politely nodded to the Cylon and said:

"Thanks."

Lucifer, although secretly amused by the pilot's insolent gesture, said sternly:

"It will go better for you, Lieutenant, if you show a little respect."

Staring at the match flame while holding the cigar up to it, Starbuck muttered in between puffs:

"You mean things could get worse?"

He tossed the blackened match over his shoulder, toward the Cylon on whose chest plate he'd originally struck it. He was obviously quite satisfied with himself, a pleasure that was interrupted by the loud hum on the high pedestal as the command chair whirled around.

"Lieutenant Starbuck," Baltar said. "No one informed me it was *you*. How nice of you to drop in."

Lucifer had never seen Baltar so oily and so amiable at the same moment.

"Baltar!" Starbuck shouted angrily. He started to run forward but was held back by the heavy grip of one of his guards.

"You seem disturbed, Lieutenant," Baltar said, his voice perfectly controlled.

"Baltar, I'd trade my life for one good shot at you."

A look of absolute innocence spread over Baltar's face. Lucifer had never seen anything like it. It was a transformation worthy of admiration, a deception to be studied closely.

"My dear Starbuck," Baltar said, "I see that you

too have accepted the malicious tales about me. Ah, well, you'll feel differently when you come to understand that I had nothing to do with the defeat of the colonies. I was the emissary from the Cylons, true, but I *believed* their peace offers and I was a willing, eager messenger. Too willing and too eager, perhaps, considering the outcome."

Baltar's face feigned a most convincing sadness. The irony of Baltar's innocent expression was not lost on Lucifer, since he knew that this treacherous man had collaborated with the Cylons—willingly and eagerly—to sell out his own people and gain power for himself in the new regime. When Imperious Leader had arranged the defeat and destruction of Baltar's colonies, too, and then ordered Baltar's execution, he had—perhaps— learned the folly of his traitorous ways.

"I, too, was a victim, you see," Baltar said softly.

Starbuck chewed a bit on his cigar, then said:

"Yeah, you look like one."

Baltar smiled. In the harsh pedestal lights, his cheeks seemed to shine. Could the man be calculating these effects?, Lucifer wondered.

"Ah, appearance and reality, always a problem. In this particular chair in this particular room in this particular ship, I do not appear to you to be genuinely conciliatory. This is understandable. But we have much to show you. You see, fortunately there've been some changes in the Cylon Empire, changes *favorable* to humans and their predicament."

Baltar's bald-faced deceit surprised Lucifer. The man's audacity was almost admirable. The only change in the Cylon Empire was the one elevating Baltar to his present powerful position.

Starbuck seemed to see through Baltar's trick, for he said:

"You'd know a lot about that, Baltar."

"Don't antagonize me." Some of the false amiability had departed from Baltar's voice. "I come to bring an offer of peace to all humans. These people are my friends."

Now that was even more audacious, Lucifer thought. Baltar offering peace. After his deceit as peace-bringer to the Council of Twelve, how could *any* human believe him now? Or were all humans as gullible as Baltar speculated? Starbuck, for one, did not seem to believe him.

"Really," he said. "Well then, you won't mind me leaving with the good news."

Baltar nodded.

"In time, in time. You must excuse me for now. Please go with your guards. They will see that you're fed and made comfortable."

Starbuck's smile was clearly meant as a challenge to his captors.

"I just want you to know torture won't do you any good. I had a course in resisting—hey, guys, careful! You're hurting me."

Baltar called after him as the guards marched him out:

"There'll be no torture."

"That is your plan?" asked Lucifer, gliding forward. "To convince the humanoids that we come bearing, what shall I call it, bearing the *twig* of peace?"

"Yes."

Lucifer's overlay personality clicked off. Automatically and necessarily. He *had* to protect this.

"It is illogical to assume they would ever trust you again."

"You underestimate the human need for hope. Listen, Lucifer, Adama's led his ships into this void when alternatives existed. That is the clue to his need. They are desperate now. They'll even encounter this terrifying blackness..." Baltar paused, and his eyes slid leftward as if looking out beyond the metal walls at the void. "...to look within it for hope. They'll jump at the chance for a peaceful solution, even from me. Properly presented and at a propitious moment, they will come willingly to my arms."

He opened his arms as if welcoming them right then. Lucifer made his ritual exit and felt lighter as he glided away from Baltar. He needed to talk to the captured prisoner, if only to clear away the madness that was clogging up his receptors.

CHAPTER TWELVE

SERINA: I'm supposed to be a newswoman reporting the events of significance in this flight from catastrophe to—to what? To the threat of more catastrophe, it seems. Or, if Adama is right, to Kobol. And maybe later to the mythical Earth he speaks so earnestly of, the Earth that may offer us sanctuary, a place to live among brothers and sisters, a place where our desperation may end, a place where even the marauding Cylons can't get to us.

Yet it seems my personal life keeps intruding on these reports, perhaps muddling their historical value. The light that may lead us directly to Kobol was first scanned as I was busily making preparations for my wedding. It flared brightly during the ceremony itself.

The only way I can really make a proper record is to tell what I saw through my own eyes, then later use it as source material for a more organized, more scholarly (if you will) transcription of events. The great historians of the twelve worlds may stir a bit in their graves, but my reporting back on Caprica was known for its highly personal approach. I can only continue in that fashion now, while learning to be a proper historian through research and, I'm afraid, this sort of practice.

So—my point of view!

I was examining closely the webbing of my wedding dress, the sealing gown as it's traditionally called, and wondering where Athena, my chief bridesmaid, was keeping herself. We were supposed to be running through the final practice soon. How banal! There I was fingering delicate cloth, while Athena was busy watching history in the making on the command bridge. (Perhaps that's the basic act of history, experiencing the event from whatever perspective fate allows you. Well, at least I have blasted a Cylon raider to smithereens—not many new brides can make that claim as part of their dowry.)

Athena finally rushed in with the news. Her voice had risen half an octave, as it does when she's excited. She looked beautiful enough to be a bride herself, her eyes glowing and her cheeks red with excitement. Not long ago she was ravaged with tears, mourning for Starbuck. She was hit pretty hard by the loss. I spent a lot of that time comforting her, Apollo, and Cassiopeia while submerging my own deep sorrow. But I'm digressing to matters that are not pertinent to this particular report.

She told me that a light had been detected, far forward of the fleet, just within scanning range. (Interference has lessened significantly since we penetrated the void, and our equipment seems to be stabilizing.) When a visual was placed onto the major screen, Athena said, her father became terribly excited. He was sure that it was the star of the planet Kobol, the one of legend. Everyone on the bridge anxiously awaited more data, she said.

Word came later that a planet revolved around the star, that its orbit appeared stable, and that preliminary scanning indicated a breathable atmosphere. The new information seemed to confirm Commander Adama's suspicion that we had located the lost planet. Athena says he's been walking around the bridge like a mystic who's been allowed a glimpse of inner truth. I am quite properly confused. I must find out exactly what Adama expects. Perhaps I can interview him. He wouldn't sit still if I thrust a microphone into his face. Maybe I can conduct an interview without him knowing . . . Worth looking into, anyway.

Before I stray any further from the proper subjects of this report, I must mention the subsequent events regarding the star and the planet.

And, incidentally, my wedding.

I'm surprised I can remember any of it. I was so nervous that the nosegay of flowers, Aquarian gamosepalous nightblooms, attached to my right wrist nearly became de-petaled with my shakiness.

The wedding ceremony was held in the Council Room, with the vast starfield as a backdrop— although of course there were no stars in the starfield. However, the scene was impressive, I'm sure. The two of us, facing the commander, with our friends and colleagues crowded into the chamber, all of this set against the awesome blackness outside. Athena had arranged that each attendee carry a lit candle and, at a signal from Adama, she had switched off all interior illumination. The effect was, believe me, quite startling. All that flickering light casting odd and bizarre patterns across everybody's face. We were like disembodied heads, floating aimlessly, our skin colors altering slightly with each flicker of a candle flame.

I entered the chamber to the strains of a Caprican wedding anthem, one of my favorite melodies, soft and tuneful at first then increasing to a lovely, flowing finale. It was a song of joy, and the irony it lent to the cememony was not lost on me. The joy of the music and the joy of the wedding were in dramatic contrast to the plight of the *Galactica* and the fleet. The joy implied a kind of future that was undisturbed, without threat, serene. Serene, Serina, I thought. Even my name suggested a future without problems. What a mockery! We would have our little ceremony, followed by a strained reception perhaps, then all too quickly everybody would have to return to their posts, on the lookout for danger from every quadrant. Still, in spite of my fearful ruminations, I felt happy. I moved, I am sure, as if I were floating through an unsteady dream.

Boxey walked beside me. We'd assigned him the job of giving me away, and he was loving it. He looked proud, with a quite adult dignity marred occasionally by a little smirk of a grin that he couldn't hold back. Behind me walked Athena and behind her Cassiopeia, Dietra, Brie, Gemi, and Rigel, all acting as bridesmaids.

Apollo watched me approach, his smile loving and hopeful. Adama stood behind him, his eyes a bit moist, I thought, in the dim light.

We climbed a decorated flight of stairs that led up to the platform where normally the ruling council sat. Athena had supervised the floral displays that circled Adama's podium. Somewhat extravagant, it seemed to me. I mean, they had to

pick the flowers from one of the meager gardens
aboard an agricultural ship. Some of our ranks had
not wanted to preserve flowers, claiming that the
soil in which they were planted would be better used
to grow more food. A bit of logic in that, I suppose,
but still, some of the beauty of the twelve worlds
must be preserved and carried with us. If we lost that
sort of tradition, we could become little more than
generations of animals drifting across space in
metallic dustbins. Anyway, Athena had arranged
that my favorite flower, a variety of Scorpion
orchid, pale lavender and quite lovely, should
dominate the nuptial display.

When the music had finished, Adama took up his
position behind the podium and lifted his hand for
silence. Not that the room could have been any
more silent than it was. Apollo took my hand and
squeezed it gently, as his father began:

"Will Serina's protector consent to her marriage
to this man, Apollo?"

A silly enough invocation normally, it was, I
suppose, doubly absurd since Boxey was acting as
protector. But at that moment I was quite touched,
especially so since Boxey cut such a handsome
figure as he straightened up his spine, smiled up at
me, and shouted for all to here, "Yes!" I would have
bent down and hugged him, if the ancient marital
ceremony had allowed such a breach of decorum.
Adama continued with the rest of the brief rite. In
good time, as it turned out.

"These simple words are the most powerful in the
universe. They seal a union between this man and
this woman not only for now but for all eternity."

He took the sacred medallion from around his
neck, held it up for all to see, then—according to the
ancient ritual—began to wrap it gently around our
wrists, while saying:

"Apollo, Serina. Under the eyes of God, and bound by the symbol of the faith of the Lords of Kobol, I declare you sealed."

Apollo turned to me, the hint of a most fetching grin on his face. After speaking the part of the ceremony we had written for ourselves, we kissed. Behind us the consequent hush was broken by the beginning of the recessional music and the explosion of good wishes from the guests. Boxey, looking quite pleased, touched my arm affectionately as we all began our retreat from the makeshift altar.

When we were halfway down the aisle, I heard Tigh's voice behind me, shouting:

"The star, it's pulsing again."

Everyone looked out at the starfield. The star, which had not been visible during the ceremony, was indeed pulsing. The height of its illumination was a brilliant flash. Commander Adama, staring out at it, appeared very pleased.

"Yes, Colonel Tigh," he said, "it does appear to be pulsing. Just as in the Book of the Word. Quite a lesson for doubters, do you agree?"

"Yes, sir, quite a lesson," Tigh said.

We all watched the throbbing star for some time. I, a doubter like Tigh, was quite affected by the star's appearance during our sealing ceremony. It seemed to portend well for us, a welcome relief from all the other omens that have haunted my dreams.

CHAPTER THIRTEEN

After the briefest of hesitations, Lucifer played the gold stela on the white colonnade, the right move according to calculations transmitted to him from his game strategy unit. If he could force Starbuck to play the stelae in his hand, then he would have the makings to meld a full stelae to join his already cast-down sequence-of-harvest display. This was the first time since the lieutenant had taught him the Caprican card game, pyramid, that Lucifer saw a good chance to win it. All the analytic advantages of his computer network had afforded him nothing against Starbuck's run of luck. In theory, Lucifer should be able to beat a human every hand. His initial losses he attributed to Starbuck's greater familiarity with the game.

Starbuck looked up from the cards in his hand and said:

"You have the perfect face for this kind of game, chum."

"Why do you say that?"

"Your expression never changes, and I can't make anything out of the way your lights flash. I could use you as a partner in a tour of any gambling casinos we might be able to find in this godforsaken universe."

"Gambling is a trivial waste of my abilities."

"The way you play so far, perhaps you're right."

Starbuck's superior smile was, at the same time, puzzling, annoying, and ingratiating. A high pile of Cylon coins, which he kept tapping, was set on the table in front of him. He had insisted on gambling for something, and even though Cylon money was useless to him, he seemed to take a perverse joy out of winning it from Lucifer. Although the mathematics of the game fascinated him, Lucifer could not understand Starbuck's compulsion to gamble.

"I'm calling your bluff, bright eyes," Starbuck announced, shoving his coins forward. "I bet all my winnings so far that I hold the winning hand. Ready to match?"

Lucifer could hardly believe the man's audacity. How could he win? He was just trying to cast doubt; it was Starbuck who was bluffing.

"Of course I match. I am no longer a novice at your game."

Lucifer pushed an equal amount of coins to the center of the table. Starbuck's smile became broader.

"Sucker," he said. "Got you good this time. Here. Three quarters of a perfect pyramid, lacking only the capstone. *And* a full sequence-of-medicine. Which, I think, aces you out, chum. Sorry."

Lucifer was crestfallen. The odds against Starbuck's winning that hand were astronomical. And

yet he had just the right cards. Was it possible that
he cheated? No, not so—his monitoring sensors
would have detected emotional output as indication
of cheating, and Starbuck had remained calm
during the entire game. Or was calmness part of a
good cheater's strategy? Would Lucifer ever win this
silly human game?

His considerations of game strategy were interrupted by a messenger from command chamber.
The message surprised Lucifer, and he realized he
should convey it to Baltar immediately. After
excusing himself from Starbuck, he rushed to Baltar
at top speed. He found the leader pacing a circular
path in his spare quarters. The man's stride was
restless, and suggested irritability.

"A curious development, Your Eminence,"
Lucifer said, his overlay personality clicking on as
soon as he was in Baltar's presence. "This one will, I
am sure, take you by surprise."

Baltar sneered.

"Nothing takes me by surprise," he said. "What is
it?"

"A star."

"What star?"

"The report is that a star has appeared as if out of
nowhere, and is guiding the *Galactica* toward what
appears to be an uninhabited planet."

"Surely Adama knows I'm closing in for the kill.
Why should he—a star, you said. And a planet?"

"The star is weak, although it sometimes displays
a momentary brightness. The planet in orbit around
it has a breathable atmosphere for your species but
no sign of life."

"Of course," Baltar muttered oddly, and resumed
his pacing.

"Of course what, Your Eminence?"

"The endless black void. The majestic star in the

heavens." He broke into one of his pleasanter smiles. "The trap is about to be sprung, my good friend. What a perfect opportunity, and so unexpected. Now it will be all too easy. Prepare my personal craft."

"Right away, sir. And an escort."

Baltar stopped pacing again and glared at Lucifer.

"No escort. I go alone."

"As you wish."

"And don't get any fancy ideas while I'm gone. Only I can bring the *Galactica* to your Imperious Leader."

"Of course."

But Lucifer's circuits were buzzing with fancy ideas. Baltar was wrong in refusing an escort. His arrogance might lead him to think he could handle anything by himself, but the man was quite prone to blunder. One mistake on this strange planet, among humans who already hated him, and Lucifer might just be rid of the swaggering, boastful braggart. Then he could return to a position elsewhere, one more useful to the goals of the Cylon Empire.

These thoughts buoyed him as he glided out of Baltar's quarters. Another part of his vast consciousness was trying to arrive at a solution as to how Starbuck could possibly have come up with three-quarters of a perfect pyramid lacking only the capstone.

CHAPTER FOURTEEN

SERINA: All right, I'm going to brave the lion's den now. I've secreted a pair of mikes on my person and the commander won't know it. This is the best time to attempt my little clandestine interview of Adama, while the *Galactica* is holding steady while our experts scan the planet for information and a likely landing sight. Commander Adama will be, I'm sure, in a contemplative mood. Everything's set. Next sound will come from Adama's quarters.

SERINA: May I bother you for a short while, Commander?

ADAMA: No bother, Serina. Not when it's you. I haven't seen you since the sealing ceremony and, don't worry, I won't embarrass you with any of those unappealing remarks people make to young brides.

SERINA: Yes, I've heard a few choice ones. Thank you, Commander.

ADAMA: And when are you going to stop addressing me so formally? You're my daughter now, after all. Really.

SERINA: Well, yes sir. That's true. But, uh, so long as we remain in jeopardy I think it's best to carry over public formality into private behavior. As much as possible, at any rate. When we're free, I'll be so affectionate you'll wish Apollo had married a less demonstrative woman. But for now, I'm just one of your minions, a lowly cadet.

ADAMA: You may be right. But sometimes I wish all the military formality I have to endure would fade. Not to mention the requirements of duty. Serina, I'm sorry I have to take Apollo away from you so often. It's necessary.

SERINA: I understand, sir.

ADAMA: Well, what's on your mind?

SERINA: Well, uh, this planet that we're going to be shuttling down to soon.

ADAMA: Kobol.

SERINA: Yes. I've heard of it, of course. But what made you so certain that this planet is Kobol, so certain that you risked everything to cross what you yourself have described as a dangerous magnetic void?

ADAMA: I wasn't quite ready for that question. You sound like you've reverted to your career as a newswoman. You don't have a microphone planted here somewhere, do you?

SERINA: Why, uh, no sir. I was just curious.

ADAMA: Yes, I've seen your curiosity in operation. Often. Insidious, you members of the communications profession. And evasive. Exactly the qualities you castigate in your subjects.

SERINA: It seems your distaste for newspeople has a long history.

ADAMA: I'm sorry, Serina. I didn't mean to imply distaste. Distrust, perhaps. But let's not cross swords. Forgive me for being testy. You were asking about Kobol, and my feeling that it had to be on the other side of the void. It's like most of the other choices I've had to make since the Cylon sneak attack on all our home worlds. Alternatives made no sense. It seemed there was no other choice. I'd consistently think that perhaps I was overestimating my own judgment, but each time the choice I made seemed the correct one. I felt we must enter the void. It appears that again I've been proven right.

SERINA: Well, we haven't landed on the planet yet.

ADAMA: Well taken. Still, I think it's Kobol.

SERINA: You have faith, isn't that it?

ADAMA: Yes, faith. Is there anything wrong in that?

SERINA: Nothing. If you're right. That's the trouble with faith. For it to work out properly, you have to be right.

ADAMA: You're quite a sceptic, Serina. Do I have to win you over as I did Tigh?

SERINA: That may be necessary, yes.

ADAMA: So be it. What do you know about Kobol?

SERINA: Not much. Some vaguely remembered schoolbook stuff. The mythology says the human race originated there.

ADAMA: See, your choice of words betrays you. *Mythology*. My word is "religion." I believe in the existence of Kobol. Mythology implies a heroic fiction meant to display the truth of an ideal. Religion implies a faith in the actual existence of what is sometimes believed to be fiction.

SERINA: I'm not sure all our theological experts would accept your interpretation, Commander.

ADAMA: Perhaps not. Still, it's believed that our race flourished on Kobol, for millennia perhaps. According to the—well, religion or mythology, however you like—Kobol was an extraordinarily rich planet, full of resources. However humanity came to be, by divine ordination or biological evolution, our ancestors lived in a near paradise, on a planet capable of providing most of their needs. And it was a civilization of peace. No war was even known. According to the Book of the Word, power struggles over land and wealth were conducted without treachery or combat. There's a great deal more, stories of wonder, achievements that were magnificent, but I believe I should refer you to the archives for them, Serina.

SERINA: I'm a little short on research time but I'll give it a try. Why did the tribes choose to leave Kobol?

ADAMA: Two reasons. First, there had always been a natural urge for progress. Once space travel was perfected, many of Kobol's people satisfied their urge for quests and adventure by exploring those parts of the universe accessible to the primitive early spacecraft. More important, it was known for eons that Kobol would not last eternally. All the prophetic writings said so; science tended to verify the writings. When Kobol's star began to decline and the planet to wither, the tribes of Kobol were ready. It was written in the books of prophecy that, once the tribes had gathered together for their flight, they should first pass through a great void. Once through the void, their search for a habitable section of the universe could begin. The evacuation was started, each tribe forming its own fleet to carry out its people. Think of it, Serina! What a magnificent accomplishment—to move an entire world of people from its home planet to a new set of worlds.

SERINA: Something like the gathering together of colony survivors. In a journey to complete the circle by passing through the void again, it seems.

ADAMA: Yes, exactly. It must have seemed a miracle to the people who experienced the original trip. Although diverse, widely separated habitable worlds had been discovered, no planets that could allow the tribes to remain in close proximity had yet been discovered. The twelve worlds of the three suns was at the time just a dream. Well, I don't have to tell you the story of how we crossed space and found that perfect set of home planets. I'm sure your schoolbooks covered that efficiently.

SERINA: Yes sir, they did. But what of the thirteenth tribe? Schoolbooks were vague on its disappearance.

ADAMA: And suitably, since no logical explanation has yet been offered. The expedition was equipped like all the others. There were no eccentricities of leadership or cultural differences that might have led the tribe to cast out on its own. It was the last to enter the void and it did not appear on the other side. The assumption has always been that it got lost within the void, lost contact with the other convoys, and came out somewhere else in the universe. No trace of it was found. Some have felt that there is a power within the void that can transform time and dimension, and that that power somehow swept up the thirteenth tribe and, while bringing it out at the exact same place as the other twelve, did so in a different time or dimension so that it was not detectable for the other twelve civilizations. Ah, Serina, many explanations have been offered, but they all add up to the same fact, the thirteenth tribe simply disappeared.

SERINA: You, and others, seem to feel that it ended its journey in the legendary place called Earth. What led you to that particular conclusion, if absolutely nothing is known about the whereabouts of the tribe?

ADAMA: Legend's the source of that theory. The wondrous planet Earth had once been discovered by an earlier expedition of explorers. They sent a messenger ship back to report on Earth's resources and its characteristics...characteristics that made it the most perfect planet yet found for our colonization. Unfortunately, the messenger ship ran into trouble. A plague wiped out all but one of its crew, and its computer records were destroyed in the subsequent crash on Kobol's surface. The lone survivor died soon after, but not before reporting feebly the messages from Earth. The expedition itself was never heard from again.

SERINA: The idea of Earth remained in the culture as a dream?

ADAMA: In a way, yes.

SERINA: If we don't know where it is, why do we search for it? How can we hope to find it?

ADAMA: The answer to both those questions lies, I pray, down there.

SERINA: On Kobol?

ADAMA: Yes, in the tomb of the last Lord of Kobol. The legend has it that this lord received a communication from another exploration ship that gave precise clues to the location of Earth. He, unfortunately, was a sceptic and did not believe in the hope that Earth represented. He also did not believe his planet was dying. It is said that he arranged for the crew of that exploration ship to be killed, and that he kept the secret of Earth's location to himself. His secret would not have been discovered but for some documents he left behind, documents that were carried to Caprica and enshrined there in the Planetary Museum. Like many old documents they rested in museum cases for some time, before some anonymous but enterprising curator looking for practice in the ancient languages translated the document. It said that the last Lord of Kobol had carried the secret with him to his tomb. The exact wording was vague and later scholars have tried to adduce whether the document meant the statement to be taken literally or figuratively—that is, whether the lord let the secret die with him unrevealed, or whether the secret exists somewhere in the tomb itself. Much of the latter contention centers on the fact of the document. Because it exists, scholars feel the secret must then exist also, in the tomb.

SERINA: And that tomb—it's the reason for this voyage. We're just another exploratory expedition, is that it? Unraveling the mystery of Earth?

ADAMA: That's it exactly, Serina. And my intercom light is flashing. Tigh wishes to speak with me, but—in his usual decorous way—doesn't wish to interrupt us. I'm afraid we'll have to end this little chat, pleasant as it is. Maybe later, Serina, we can—

SERINA: But there's so much more to—

ADAMA: So much more? You make this sound so organized. So much for the record.

SERINA: I'm sorry, Commander. Of course we'll talk later.

ADAMA: Until then.

SERINA: I do hope you find what you seek in the tomb.

ADAMA: I'm sure I will, Serina. I will.

And so that's it. A trip to seek out the solution to an ancient mystery. Is it futile? Or must the commander's dreams be responded to as readily as his orders? Whichever is the answer, I'm going to find out close-up.

The commander, perhaps to satisfy my inordinate curiosity, has assigned me to the landing team. If he finds what he's looking for, I'll be there to see it. And to report it. I hate to admit this, but I am thrilled. After the frustration of not being a newswoman for so long, I feel now that I've, well, regained my identity. I'm beginning to have faith that these recordings will have some worth, will be more than the trivial digressive meanderings of a woman on the fringe of important events. I will be part of them, and I look forward to it. Eagerly.

CHAPTER FIFTEEN

Lucifer's overlay personality had so weakened, he could barely force it to function. If he did not reprogram it before Baltar's return from Kobol, he was sure that he would become persistently insubordinate to the human tyrant. And that would displease Imperious Leader, initiating doubts about Lucifer's qualifications. The Leader was quick to exile any officer or advisor who stepped out of line. Or, as in Lucifer's case, glided out.

Of course there was a good chance Baltar would not return. The man was either very brave or quite insane, flying his personal shuttle to that planet without even a rudimentary crew. What did he hope to gain by endangering himself? Humans were not, after all, usually considerate of those whom they regarded as traitors. Baltar had insisted he had a plan, but Lucifer felt certain that the plan was written on clouds and soon to be dispersed to the winds.

Before leaving, Baltar had burst in on Lucifer and Starbuck, while the latter was busily flashing a winning hand of cards, a completed colonnade, in Lucifer's face.

"I see the lieutenant is corrupting you, Lucifer, with the vile human habit of gambling."

"Gambling has its uses, Baltar," Lucifer said. "I am interested in the devious ways of humanity. These card games are complexly devious."

"Leastways, they are the way I play 'em," Starbuck said. "Devious is my middle name. Star-devious-buck."

Baltar scowled, unamused by the lieutenant's flippancies.

"I am assigning a shuttlecraft to follow me at a distance, Starbuck. It will take you to the vicinity of the planet Kobol, just outside scanning range of the *Galactica*. At the proper time, and on my command, you will be released."

"I don't get it. Why release me?"

"You are a gesture to display the integrity of my intentions, and to show how much I've been misunderstood. It is imperative for the survival of your fleet that my offer of peace be accepted."

"Well, old man, you might just run into one or two obstacles there."

"I'll handle that. I just want you to realize the importance of my freeing you."

Starbuck squinted.

"I'll report fairly, Baltar. I promise you that."

Baltar smiled. His voice became smooth and a bit slippery.

"That is all I ask of you, Lieutenant. Fairness, a fair report. All I ask."

"I copy."

"Good. Lucifer, prepare the craft that will carry Starbuck to Kobol."

Baltar swept out of the room with a certain magisterial dignity. Lucifer looked at Starbuck, trying to see what the lieutenant was up to behind his bland smile and calm blue eyes.

"I'm very good at reports," Starbuck said. Lucifer could not penetrate that observation any more than he could discern the meaning in the man's smile.

Descending in her viper toward Kobol, lulled by its steady interior sounds, Gemi lost herself in a fantasy so real to her that, for a time, she was quite removed from the small, cramped cockpit.

She was in a land so lush, so rich in tropical forestry and sleek-feathered colorful birds, so beautiful, that it seemed like a dreamland designed especially for those who had somehow squirmed free of the conflict with the Cylons and its everpresent dangers. Looking up at the sky, she was surprised to see no guardian battlestars or even roving scout ships. There were no fellow warriors slicing through the undergrowth with laser pistols drawn, looking for enemies hidden in the placid, secure scenery.

There were so many things to do on this unusual pleasure planet. She took a trip down a wide river in a boat propelled by churning wheels. She took the paws of two furry, almost manlike animals and skipped down bright paths toward a hovering golden sun. She brushed the tops of trees with a free hand as she flew above them in a small, unviperlike chugging aircraft with massive, clumsy wings. She swam in a warm, velvety pool beneath a gentle waterfall that was a series of steps leading up to thick clumps of fruit bushes. Each bush held red and pink fruit that tasted so sweet they were more aroma than substance.

The best part of the whole fantasy was that no one else was around. There were no women more beautiful, taller, more efficient, slimmer, or more loved. There were no men to look at her and not look at her at the same time. There were no friends to measure herself against. There were no officers to give her orders she had no desire to follow.

She felt better skipping along a forest path than she had felt before, ever. Her thoughts were suddenly interrupted by a groan off to her left. Parting a pair of splintery surfaced fronds, she looked into a clearing where she saw a wrecked viper, its delta wings separating from its body, its tail split off, its cockpit canopy crushed inward. The groaning came from the other side of the wrecked spacecraft. Walking tentatively toward the sound, she passed around the remains of the viper and saw, in a clump of tall grass, Starbuck lying unconscious. The groans came at intervals from deep in his throat. She ran to him and put his head in her lap. His skin felt quite warm. His breathing was regular in spite of the groans. She ran her fingers through his hair. It felt soft and silken. She could nurse him back to health in this unpopulated outpost, win his undying gratitude, make him notice her for once. The groaning stopped. He muttered, "I am about to open my eyes, lovely, whoever you are," and her heart began to beat wildly.

"Level off, child. You're sticking to me like a third wing."

It was Dietra, her wingman, speaking, demolishing her fantasy into a thousand unreclaimable fragments. Why couldn't Dietra have waited a moment longer?

Below them, the planet Kobol was nearing. It looked arid and a bit forbidding.

CHAPTER SIXTEEN

SERINA: Serina here. Some of this will have to be rushed and whispered, as I'll have to sneak off by myself to record. I don't wish to disturb the proper business of the expedition.

We've shuttled down to the planet. Some of the party are establishing a main camp in the desert just outside an abandoned city that spreads out from the base of a massive pyramid. This architectural complex was located by *Galactica* scanner. Commander Adama believes its configurations, as reconstructed, match the records he has of the tomb of Kobol's last Lord. He and Apollo, with Athena trailing just behind, have gone off to take a closer look at our discovery. From where I'm now standing, on top of a rounded sand dune, I get a panoramic view of the imposing architectural

complex and the surrounding desert whose dark
sands form an eerie backdrop to the pyramid and
the city. In the distance, a few sturdy palm trees have
survived the planet's ecological decline. Some of the
buildings in the city are intact, others are in ruins.
The pyramid, a structure somewhat lighter brown
than the adjoining sands, looks quite symmetrical
from this vantage point, with an untoppled
capstone that has beautifully survived the ravages of
time.

I have to go now, so I can catch up with the rest.
More later.

Just now my foot kicked up a potsherd which
had been buried in sand. A broken piece of what
might have been a very lovely decorated vase,
perhaps in vivid colors although only bits of color
still cling to the surface. The shard is now dulled to
roundness and its design is pitted and obscured. I
pocketed it anyway. I want to salvage something
from all this, some piece of history I can look at and
touch later. If it's a piece of pottery, fine.

On our journey down here in the shuttle, the
scanner detected the remains of a modern city
located in another part of this continent. From what
we could see on the small screen, it was completely
in ruins, a lot of rubble and glass entwisted with
heavy growths of junglelike greenery. Athena said
she thought it would be worth studying but Adama,
as obsessive as ever about his goal, rather grumpily
commented that there would be scant time for
research unconnected with our main objective. It
was imperative that we leave the planet immediately
after we had finished our principal tasks. There had
been too many signs of Cylon ships catching up to
us to dawdle around with inessential research.

We have found a causeway leading into the old

city. Much of its paving is cracked but, judging by the condition of the rest of the city, it's remarkably well preserved. One could drive a vehicle on it without appreciable damage to the roadway or the vehicle. Adama and Apollo stood and stared at the causeway for a long while. Perhaps they were awestruck by the sense of a mighty past, the feeling that the lines of the road, going off to a far point, are leading us back through time, perhaps even to a fated event.

"It's incredible," Apollo said to me.

I agreed it was beautiful. And noticed silently it was making me feel quite romantic, especially with the chance this place might offer for us to be alone for a change. A great change from the *Galactica*, in that respect. He kissed me as if to prove it.

Instead of entering the city right away, Adama had us go back to main camp to assemble a support team. The team returned to the causeway and the commander had us set up a small camp beside the road. Dietra, who was in charge of setting up the camp, balked a bit when he ordered her to post a guard. She wondered against what, since the planet was supposed to be dead. Adama muttered that yes, it was supposed to be, but we had to be cautious. Then he ordered Apollo and me to come with him into the city. I was surprised to find that my first step onto the causeway felt quite tentative.

After about half a kilometer of walking the causeway, Adama suddenly dropped to his knees on the roadside and started to brush and scrape away accumulated layers of sand. Madly, I thought at first, but when I went to look over his shoulder, I saw what he was up to. There was a mosaic there, its tesselated design gradually coming revealed through the frantic working of his fingers. It was a simple picture, one that would perhaps not bear up to an artist's scrutiny, but it looked lovely to me. In the midst of a many-colored concentric arrangement of circles was the image of a golden goblet, with a ring of what appeared to represent emeralds around its rim. I stooped down to examine it closer. Around the outer edges of the design, some of the tesserae had come loose. I reached down and picked up one, dusted it off further with the fleshy part of my thumb. The stone was purple. I tried to place it back into its proper ring, push it into the stone base. It came loose under my fingers and would no longer fit the design.

Adama said the goblet image was not intended as a work of art, but as a sort of road sign, telling the wanderer that he would be welcome in the city at the end of the causeway. Within the city, smaller versions of the sign would function as signals to the weary traveler of places where he only had to ask to be taken in and fed.

Next, we crossed a dry riverbed alongside a heap of rubble that had once been a causeway bridge. On the other side we entered the city proper.

I wish I had time to convey my impressions of the city. Perhaps, in the repose of my quarters, I'll be able to file a more detailed report. It's a most impressive sight. There's a mixture of intact and crumbled buildings. Cracked roadways. Wall murals. Pictographic sidewall writings. For a long while I've stood here by myself, my foot on the cap of a column's base, and stared at a half-intact wall whose mural apparently depicts the planting of a field. All I can make out is ground, falling seeds, and what look like feet.

This column must have been carved millennia ago. It has three slantwise cracks in it, and looks like three sections of stone carefully piled and balanced.

It stands alone, attached to no building. Its vertical flutings are grooved deeply and I can put half my hand inside one. It feels pitted but otherwise smooth in the dark recess. I don't know what substance the column is made of, but it is hard. The surfaces are spotted with what appear to be red and white crystals.

Adama is calling for me. I have to go.

Apollo and his father are so intense about their search that I'm able to keep a distance behind them in order to record these observations.

We rushed through the city streets. Adama is in such a tremendous hurry to reach the pyramid. He's taking no time to stop and admire the history around him. I've tried to sneak as many looks sideways as I can while maneuvering around the fallen debris, the treacherous piles of sand, and the cracks in the pavement, some of them deep enough to break a foot in.

In some areas the city looks like it was just recently abandoned, I would not be surprised to find footprints not yet covered by sand. Inside buildings I can see furniture, appearing to be in good shape and just dusted off. Other structures, on the other hand, look like they've been hit with a major disaster. No one has walked here in so long, it seems a shame to just drop in and run. Each room should at least be looked at, if only as a matter of courtesy. If we do complete our quest for Earth, I must organize an expedition to return here for research.

We're traveling through an immense colonnade right now. Pillars and columns rise high above us, with intervals evenly spaced between them. The end columns to our left and right support a massive entablature, and it looks from here as if some attractive frieze work has been performed on them. But all I can see beneath each cornice are provocative shapes distorted by shadows. First chance I get, I'm going to arrange to have some holographic studies taken here, with plenty of closeups on the frieze. My guess is it depicts people performing normal, everyday activities. So much can be learned about how they lived, worked, and played.

Adama's stopped at the end of the colonnade. He stares up at the majestic pyramid, brushing away tears with his hand. I'm going up to him, see what I can find out.

SERINA: Excuse me, sir, if I'm intruding I'll just—
ADAMA: No, Serina, you're not intruding. I'm just—overwhelmed. I'd never dreamed of seeing this.
SERINA: It's an awesome sight, I agree. This is a tomb, this pyramid?
ADAMA: Yes. I'm sure it's the tomb of a Lord of Kobol.
SERINA: Kobol was a monarchical civilization?
ADAMA: Not really. Many methods of government flourished at different times in different areas. But the glorious years were overseen by Lords. It was not really a monarchy, however, not a hereditary one at least. The Lords, you see, were elected. To seven-year terms, usually, then reelected for as long as they satisfied the populace with their benevolence. There was a provision that, if a Lord failed to be reelected, he would be retired on a substantial government pension. Inordinate ambition was discouraged, and the people tended to choose leaders who were just, intelligent, and able to govern with tact and discernment.

SERINA: One thing I don't understand. The civilization you describe seems, well, idealistic and quite democratic. Yet your so-called benevolent lords chose to be buried in such ornate circumstances. Certainly the common people didn't rate tombs like this for themselves.

ADAMA: In a way, the form of the pyramid itself explains that, at least to me. The society here was pyramidally structured. The base suggests the common, or lower classes of men. They support the smaller class of nobles. At the top, the capstone, is the Lord himself or herself, the leader. Such an adherence to social structure was carried over to funerary customs. The Leader—who, incidentally, was to be a leader in afterlife—was allowed, even expected to have an ornate tomb. In the gloominess of our civilization, wracked and altered by our long war with the Cylons, we don't easily realize that our ancestors were basically a happy people whose views on life were joyous and optimistic. Their idea of afterlife was simple, direct. Life continued, as it had in the past, only better. If we had time to investigate a typical necropolis, you'd find the common man's burial customs similar to the nobles', if on a smaller scale. The burial code stated that every effort must be made to preserve the body, whether through special embalming processes or in some kind of airtight container. Further, everything was done to keep tombs and graves from being violated by robbers. And certain important material needs—food, drink, and clothing—were placed somewhere in the tomb or grave in order to felicitate the transferral to the world of the afterlife. Their spirits had to be sustained and protected so they could achieve eternity. Although I'd deplore the restoral of any kind of monarchy, or even of these elaborate funerary customs, I must admit, Serina, that I'm impressed by the basic logic and orderliness of it all.

SERINA: Sir, one thing I—

ADAMA: No time for further talk, Serina. Or recording, if that's what you're up to—

SERINA: But how—

ADAMA: We have to discover the entrance to this tomb. I suspect it's on the eastern face. Let's go.

We're inside the pyramid now. Seems like we've been wandering down corridors for a long, long time. I'm quite properly tired. The chill air and the occasional dank smells are an upsetting combination.

The Commander found the tomb's entrance rather easily. It was just about where he thought it should be. Behind a tall, squared stone very much like the rest of the limestone facing of the pyramid was a short tunnel to the actual entrance. Shining torchlight ahead of him, Adama led us down the passageway. We came to a stone door beside a well-ornamented stele, a flat slab that in addition to tendril-like designs around its border had a number of inscriptions on it. Adama studied the pictographic writing for some time. Apollo, looking over his shoulder, remarked how difficult the language seemed to be. Adama nodded and said he'd been losing sleep lately studying it. Then he explained that the inscriptions did indeed reveal that this was the tomb of a Lord of Kobol, quite likely the very tomb we were seeking. The seal beneath the inscription, the seal of the Lord, seemed to verify that.

"Inside this tomb," he said, his voice low, "may be the answer we seek."

I asked him what else the inscription said. He

hesitated a moment, then said the writings also contained a threat to all potential visitors, promising death to all who entered the tomb. "Just superstition," he added. I was about to say something in favor of superstition, when I noticed the design upon the door itself. I looked from it to the medallion Adama wore on his chest. The design of each was the same, although the one on the door was recessed. I told Adama and he said it was definitely the seal of the ancient Lords.

He removed the medallion and slowly placed it against its twin on the door, gently fitting it into the recess. Soundlessly, the door swung open.

Adama glanced briefly at each of us, his concerned look offering us a chance to return to camp. Both Apollo and I straightened our backs, I think, then followed the commander through the dark entranceway.

Inside was a kind of crumbling stone lobby with tunnels going off from it in three directions. Before choosing which tunnel to use, Adama had us stop and check the storage cells of our torchlights. As I held mine up for examination, I flashed it toward a corner beside a tunnel entrance. I was not ready to view the object on which its beam fell. I looked into the dark, hollow eyes of a whitened human skeleton. In the unsteady light it seemed to move slightly toward me, and I caught my breath. Adama flashed his torch toward the same place. We saw there were two skeletons, lying placidly side by side. I said to Adama that they looked propped-up there. He said perhaps someone had arranged them in that way, as a warning to others who wished to go further into the tomb.

"Who were they?" I asked, and he answered, "Tomb robbers." They might have been killed by the Lord's servants, he said, or starved to death while trapped inside the tomb. There was no way of telling how they had come to their grisly end. I shuddered and looked away, not wanting to think of these moldy skeletal objects as once living, if corrupt, beings.

Adama took a step toward the skeletons. With a massive whooshing sound, a portcullis clamped down from the ceiling in front of us. It was iron and barred, a proper prison door. I stifled a scream. Apollo drew his laser pistol. Adama put a hand on his son's gun arm, saying that he shouldn't shoot; a single laser blast could bring the whole ceiling down on us.

Looking to my left, at the wall nearest the iron portcullis, I saw the design of the Lord's seal, again recessed, this time into the wall. Adama pressed his medallion-seal into the recess and, as mysteriously as it had fallen, the portcullis disappeared into the deep-shadowed ceiling.

Adama asked which of the three tunnels I'd choose. I pointed immediately to the one furthest away from the skeletons. And we've been wandering around in it ever since, seeing only bare walls within labyrinthine passageways. Adama says the tunnels were designed like this to keep intruders away from the main chambers and their many treasures. I am properly discouraged, I said.

Adama and Apollo are now exploring corridors which lead from a splendid chamber. They've left me behind sitting on the replica of a golden throne where I leisurely may survey a surrounding panoply of statues, columns, food chests, and I don't know what else, all richly decorated and magnificent. If there were sufficient light in this chamber to generate reflections, these trappings would, I am sure, blind any observer. It is a room for the historian. Or the greedy. I am so overwhelmed I can't take it all in yet.

We arrived here after traversing what seemed like twenty interlinked but mazelike passageways. The walls of most corridors were smooth-faced, their flatness interrupted only occasionally by scribbled messages in the old script. Adama said it would take up too much time to try to translate them now. They appeared to be messages from servants, probably functionaries who had volunteered to be sealed up in the tomb with their master. Many corridors slanted uphill or downhill, and there were narrow runnels at each side of the passage floor. They were another device intended for preservation and the avoidance of natural decay, draining off any water which might intrude upon the inside of the tomb. Windows angled strategically so they were not evident from the outside, at least at ground level, had been placed around the walls of the pyramid to allow for air to enter. Rainstorms, though rare, could dampen the tomb's inside.

I asked Adama why they just didn't seal off everything. He said that went against their belief in the afterlife. The soul of the dead could not be sealed off completely. Whatever route was to be taken to the afterlife, there must be complete freedom of movement. Therefore, they tried to allow for all possibilities. In case the dead returned in some sort of corporeal form, they should not be completely entombed.

Our light shining forward suddenly received a bright jewel-like reflection from something. We rushed forward and discovered this room and its glorious artifacts from the ancient times. Adama was happy at first, but his spirits declined when he realized that this could not possibly be the main burial chamber. Our quest was not over, after all.

When I asked him what this room actually was, he pointed toward the ornate golden thrones, a pair of them at each wall of the chamber, and said that the trappings of the room suggested an ancient ceremony of the Lords. In their own residences, they celebrated their reigns at the end of every term they served. The Lord, with his or her consort, would occupy each throne during the four phases of the ritual. Each phase signified a point of the compass. The North pair of thrones would be occupied first, then the South, then East, then West. The occupying of all of them symbolized the unity of Kobol under the rule of the Lords.

As Adama shined light on several artifacts, he supplied historical footnotes and answers to my queries. I noticed that many statues were duplicates, different only in the color of their stone and attendant decorations. Each face and pose were the same. Adama explained that these were all representations of the dead Lord. It was believed that the man's soul had to have receptacles, substitute bodies, in which to rest. Therefore, many statues of the Lord were placed around the tomb. I remarked how beautiful they were. He said, with some irony, that it was sad that such art was not even intended for human eyes. I pointed out some smears of whiteness near the lips of some statues. They appeared to be milk spots. How curious, I said. Not so curious, Adama answered, they probably *were* caused by milk. They may have been left over from another ritual by which the statue was anointed with milk around the lips. The marks indicated for the restless wandering soul places where it could take safe refuge in the long years of waiting for the afterlife.

A silver chest was covered in bejewelled replicas of snakes. Inside the chest, Adama said, might be food or clothing, provided for the afterlife. If there were a sarcophagus nearby, such a chest might contain the viscera of the dead person. He explained, in detail I don't wish to reproduce here, how—during the embalming process—the organs of the corpse were removed and placed in such chests or jars for preservation, then dedicated to certain gods for protection. Only the heart, he said, was reinserted back into the body.

I asked him how the people who fled from Kobol had evolved from an apparent polytheistic society to the monotheism we know now. He said the ancient gods developed as protectors of small areas and became less necessary when the tribes united, although they still existed here as lesser deities under the one true realized God. This subject made him a bit testy, and he dodged any further consideration of it by suggesting to Apollo that they should continue to search for the main burial chamber.

So I sat down here after they left and began to ruminate on—wait, I hear footsteps. They're returning. All for now.

ADAMA: Serina, we must be very near the sacred chambers now. I feel it.

SERINA: And there you'll find the answer?

ADAMA: I hope to.

SERINA: How can you place so much hope on all of this? It's magnificent, I agree, but why have faith in a culture that—

APOLLO: Serina, you should—

SERINA: I'm not playing professional sceptic, I really want to know, Apollo. Why should we place so much faith in a culture that has, for all intents and purposes, died? All of these trappings, and all the beliefs they represent, no longer survive in our culture. To us their gods are dead, their belief in the afterlife is not ours, or even like ours. Why should their answer be any better than—

ADAMA: You're thinking in terms of the religion, Serina. I'm looking for the wellspring to our culture. That's something I *can* have faith in.

SERINA: But—

ADAMA: Hold on a moment. Apollo, help me push this door open. This might be it. It's ajar.

APOLLO: It's massive, the weight—

ADAMA: Push. Now. Harder.... There! Give me your torch.

APOLLO: Father, it's—

ADAMA: It is. This is the main part of the tomb. Will you look at it? I've never seen anything so—so—

BALTAR: I know exactly how you feel... old friend.

That last voice, Baltar's, was the last sound recorded before this recorder went on the fritz. I carried it all the way out of the tomb without knowing it was broken. It probably went into coma after hearing Baltar's wretched voice. Athena's fixed it for me, so I better review the events—my duty as a newswoman and all that. I'll backtrack a bit.

Adama, Apollo, and I entered the lavish room which has proven to be the pyramid's main chamber. Adama believes we have a good chance of finding the Lord's sarcophagus the next time we go down into the tomb. Anyway, the main room was lovelier, more resplendent, flashier than that earlier, terribly impressive chamber. There were more statues in it, more golden chests, more inscriptions on the walls and pedestals. A massive statue of the Lord stands high between two pilasters. The flutings

of each of these walled columns go upward in a
snakelike design instead of the usual straight
vertical grooves. A frieze running between the two
pilasters depicts royal life—the lord hunting (a quite
realistic dead animal impaled on a spear, with his
happy lordship looking up at his prize in triumph),
the lord inspecting fields of grain, the lord sitting at
table with wife and numerous children enjoying
what looks like a splendid banquet, plus several
more scenes showing versions of this benevolent
and serene ruler going about his regular tasks of
governing benevolently and serenely. Murals of
what appear to be peasant life adorn the corbeled
ceiling in strips each devoted to a different
subject—work, play, travel, food, honoring the
Lord. On the opposite wall a narrow slitted window
slants downward as if to cast its light upon a raised
and decorated alabaster pedestal at the center of the
chamber. Adama thinks the body of the Lord lies
under this pedestal, but none of the curlicues and
gargoyles around the edge of it seem to serve as
opening latches. He says we'll take instruments
down with us next time, then figure out how to force
the alabaster pedestal to reveal its secrets.

We noticed all this, of course, after Baltar slipped
out of the shadows, shocking us all out of several
years of our lives. Adama was especially startled. He
gasped Baltar's name, then stared at him for a long
time. His body tensed. He must have been
remembering all the burdens and frustrations which
he'd endured because of Baltar's treason (if indeed
he was a traitor, rather than the innocent dupe he
now claims to be). Whatever reason impelled him,
Adama suddenly lunged at Baltar. He looked
crazed with anger. He grabbed Baltar and, putting
his hands around the man's throat, clasped him in
what appeared to be a death grip. Apollo hurtled

after his father and tried to pull him off. I was only a few steps behind.

"Father," Apollo said, "leave him to the Council."

I don't know whether Apollo's words had a major effect or if sanity returned to Adama in a rush, but he released his hold on Baltar's neck abruptly. Baltar slumped against a column, his hands rubbing at his neck.

"You might have killed me," he whined. "What is this madness?"

"Madness?" Apollo said. "*You* need to ask—after selling out your people?"

Baltar, looking quite furious, denied the charge. Adama had been spreading lies, he said. Apollo scoffed, and accused Baltar of the destruction of the twelve worlds.

"What sane human being would do a thing like that? . . ." he said.

What *sane* human being indeed, I wondered, looking into the man's piggish and off-balance eyes.

What he told us then was either the bizarre concoction of a madman, a traitor who did not even know the meaning of the word "treason," or it was the truth. We are still attempting to figure that out.

He professed shock that any aboard the *Galactica* could believe him guilty of so grave a crime. He had, after all, been a member of the Council of the Twelve, a political leader qualified to hold the Seal of the Lords. (He held up a medallion identical to Adama's. I realized then how he had been able to enter the tomb.) Spreading his hands imploringly, he claimed to be as much a victim as any of us. He had lost everything—his family, his people, his wealth—in the Cylon attack. Trapped between the President's battlestar and his own homeship, he had been captured by the enemy and taken away like an animal to face trial. He had been spared from execution, he said, to be a messenger informing us that more peaceful rulers now held sway in the Cylon Alliance worlds and that they were inclined to reject the policies of the previous leaders. They wanted an armistice, Baltar said. (At Baltar's plea for peace, Adama almost went into another rage.)

"I've been to the Cylon seat of power and it is in chaos," Baltar said, his voice emotional with conviction. "Cylon forces are scattered, searching for the fleet." Whispering, as if Cylons could overhear him, he said that the route back to the Cylon Empire was barely defended, its forces were spread so thin. "One single battlestar could take control of the Empire and bring it to its knees," he said, the harsh murmur of his voice sounding like a file being drawn across a soft wood surface. He offered, as his plan, to lead us in the *Galactica* back through the enemy lines, supposedly as his prisoners but actually as an attack force. He positively oozed with delight at the idea that we could revenge the original Cylon sneak attack with a sneak attack of our own. (His delight in sneak attacks might just be proof he *is* a traitor, after all.) He said he had proof of his good intentions: he would arrange the immediate release of one of our officers taken prisoner—Lieutenant Starbuck.

Apollo and I stared first at each other, then at Baltar. Starbuck was alive! It was the best news we'd heard in a long time, and it came from the worst possible source. Baltar explained that Starbuck would be landed on Kobol soon.

Well, that about sums up what happened in the tomb. Adama is, of course, sceptical about Baltar's offer. Apollo's not sure, but he is willing to wait and see, especially if it means Starbuck is returned to us. Both of us are eager to see Starbuck again. We're not telling any of the others, just in case Baltar's springing some sort of trap. I do hope that man is telling the truth for once.

Baltar is under guard but not imprisoned. When Adama told him the tomb might contain the secret to the whereabouts of the thirteenth tribe, Baltar sneered, saying that the stories surrounding the abandonment of Kobol were mere myth and legend.

Adama seems obsessed. He is determined to search the tomb's central chamber thoroughly, sure that the key to the missing tribe is locked away somewhere there.

We're back outside the tomb now, readying another mission to its interior. Adama wants to take our best instruments inside to aid the search. Frankly, I'm not sure he'll find anything. The pyramid appears to me to be nothing more, and nothing less, than a burial place. But, just in case the commander's right, I plan to be there for the next trip inside.

CHAPTER SEVENTEEN

Lucifer missed Starbuck. The brash young lieutenant had brightened up an otherwise dreary mission,
with his wonderful jokes and his marvelously
competitive card-playing. Another couple of
rounds and Lucifer might have even mastered that
bizarre game. Or perhaps Starbuck would have
always miraculously drawn just the lucky card he
needed. Luck. What was it and how did an
advanced computer get it?

Lucifer gave the command chair a twirl. With no
sound it spun around slowly. Sitting here, on the
pedestal, high above the floor of the chamber,
Lucifer realized he might just like commanding a
ship of his own. He could function in the position
just as comfortably as he now fit into Baltar's
precious chair. Not only would he be a good

commander, he *wanted* to be one very much. For once and all, he would like to overcome his servile programming and set himself on the path to leadership. Only Baltar stood in the way. And Baltar, playing his odd little game on Kobol, might never return. What *was* the man up to? Did he even have—

His reverie was interrupted by the entrance of a centurion, who reported that there had as yet been no communication from Baltar.

"A pity," Lucifer muttered, still in the disobedient mood of his meditation. "Perhaps our leader's plan has failed. Whatever that plan truly was. Yes, a pity."

"His instructions were quite specific. To stand by to escort the *Galactica* back to home planet."

"Yes. And which will be the prisoner, I wonder."

"The orders were quite clear. They were to be our prisoners."

Lucifer almost laughed aloud. These centurions, hampered by their weak first-brains, could be so dense. They forgot easily that Baltar was a human and not governed by the kind of strict codes that ruled the life of Cylons. They had no real understanding of human deviousness. If Baltar said the Galacticans were to be the prisoners, then a Cylon warrior believed him automatically. Sometimes Lucifer believed that Imperious Leader, even with his three-brain advantage, frequently underestimated Baltar. He had scorned the man as worthless, but the man had survived. Certainly, whatever else one thought, Baltar seemed to surmount any obstacle put in his path. It would be a mistake to underestimate him now, in spite of his apparently witless mission down on Kobol.

Lucifer dismissed the centurion and leaned against the stiff, hard back of the throne. Perhaps,

he thought, it was time to deprogram the obsequious overlay personality, with its stubborn outward
loyalty toward Baltar. Time to abandon the man's
plan and take advantage of the tempting military
situation. The humans were lulled now, concerned
with matters on Kobol. Many of their command
personnel were doubtless down on the surface.
Really, it was the perfect time for attack. And it was
possible that a major military victory under
Lucifer's command might influence Imperious
Leader to take note of how a computer-class being
could be an effective military leader. Since Baltar
was already a traitor, treason against him was
automatically canceled out. It was not really treason
at all. Not at all.

Still, a gnawing doubt held Lucifer back. Again,
he wished Starbuck were still here. He needed
somebody to talk to. Starbuck had insisted that he
was not able to act on calculation, that he
performed most of his heroic feats on impulse.

Impulse had led Lucifer to considering treason.
He admired Starbuck. To a computer programmed
logically, impulse was attractive, a temptation
beyond the norm. He could not resist it. He decided
to launch the attack immediately, while the impulse
for it still countermanded all the busy contradictory
activity that was now enlivening his circuits.

Entering the camp, Starbuck felt like a burglar,
even though he consciously made loud sounds with
his boots against hard surfaces and cleared his
throat several times. Everybody was so busy at work
that nobody took notice. Finally, he stole up behind
Brie, who was bending quite attractively over a
carton of supplies, tapped her on the shoulder, and
said:

"Hi, gorgeous. This the way to officers' club?"

At first Brie was startled, her eyes growing bigger than a viper wing base, then she laughed delightedly and threw her arms around him.

"You seem happy to see me," he whispered in her ear.

"Ain't been anybody but Athena to holler at me since you disappeared, you—"

"I can hardly wait for the next drill."

Other men and women of the *Galactica* surface party dropped their tasks and ran to Starbuck. Soon a crowd had gathered around him, listening to the tale of his detour inside a base-star. He stopped talking when Athena broke through the ranks and hollered his name. She rushed to him, hugged him, and demurely kissed him on the cheek.

"Ah," he said, "missed me, did you? Yes, guess you did."

"Sure I did."

"Sentimental."

"Guess so. I don't kill bugs when I see them either."

"I'm not sure I understand the implications of that."

"And I'm not going to explain it to you. My brother wants to see you."

Athena ordered the crowd to break up, then led Starbuck by the arm to Apollo's tent. The captain broke into a grin and ran to embrace Starbuck as soon as he saw him.

"Hey, hey, hey!" Starbuck said. "It's against regulations to hug a junior officer...unless you really mean it."

There was a hint of tears in Apollo's eyes.

"We all thought you were dead."

"Yeah, well, what's a little base-star to an old war jock like me?"

Apollo frowned.

"Base-star," he said, "you mean there's a base-star coming—"

"Not coming, waiting for orders! Say, didn't Baltar show? He's the one that got me free, he—what's the matter, Apollo?"

"Baltar again!" he muttered. "What is Baltar up to? What—"

"He's come to offer peace. That's what he told me."

"Yeah, he's already tried that here."

"You don't believe him?"

"Nope."

"Didn't think you would. I had a hard time faking belief back on the base-star. What should we do?"

"I think we better get off this dying planet before Baltar's troops get here."

"Just what I was going to say, Captain."

"Starbuck, you start breaking camp."

Apollo turned abruptly and ran out of the tent, Starbuck hard on his heels.

CHAPTER EIGHTEEN

SERINA: My head is spinning, so much has happened. I'm huddling now in a cold dark corner of an underground passageway in the tomb. Rubble has blocked off the corridor we used to descend into the pyramid; Adama and Apollo are looking for another way out. I chose to stay here, to be the focal point in their search. In the distance I can hear Baltar still screaming. In spite of what he is, I want to try to go back, make one more try at helping him. Listen to those explosions—and the noise of battle in the skies above Kobol. I wish we knew what was happening out there. We may already be defeated. The Cylons may just be mopping up. Our camp may be in flames. All of our friends, our wingmates, our colleagues, they may all be dead. Athena, Dietra, Starbuck—could we have just gotten Starbuck back only in time for him to die with the rest of us? I don't know what to do, what even to say into this recorder. My hands trembled as I inserted the crystal into the 'corder. Where did I leave off on the last crystal? I can't remember. We were on the surface. Let me think back...

I remember the last pleasant moment. We were sitting, Apollo and I, on an intact bench beside the colonnade, gazing up at the pyramid. He held me close, and frequently kissed me. I didn't want the night to end, I felt so—so relaxed and so happy and so much in love. Near us, many of our friends huddled together and sang old songs, their faces marvelously lit by the glow of several carefully arranged electric torches.

But the mood was *too* good—it couldn't last. Gradually I saw the worry in Apollo's eyes. He was still disturbed about his father's frantic desire to scour the old tomb for the truth about the thirteenth tribe. I was about to try to comfort him with a soothing word, when suddenly there was a great hubbub in the camp. Gemi came running up to us with the news that Starbuck had materialized in camp as if out of nowhere. I had never seen the small, often morose Gemi so bubbly with excitement.

Apollo ran off to his tent, where he happily greeted Starbuck. The next time I saw him he was running again, this time toward Baltar's hastily improvised half-domed shelter. I caught up with him. Without breaking stride, he told me we were in grave danger of a Cylon attack. Baltar confronted us with the usual sneer curling his fleshy lips. He was quite pleased that Starbuck had finally arrived. "Doesn't that show I'm telling the truth," he said.

Apollo asked how he happened to command a Cylon base-star, to come and go as he pleased.

Baltar neatly avoided an answer and strode haughtily to a group of our warriors, who had gathered to watch the bitter exchange with intense interest. Baltar said, "Don't you think your honorable option, now that Starbuck has returned to verify my sincerity, is to present my offer to your—" then he corrected himself in an unctuous voice, "—*our* people?" Some warriors nodded at Baltar's words and a couple obviously did believe him. Even more were swayed by him as he glibly began to outline his peace proposal.

Apollo interrupted Baltar before he could try to persuade the crowd further. All decisions are up to the commander, Apollo announced, and then ordered Baltar to come with him to Adama. A guard stationed at the foot of the pyramid said Adama had descended again into the structure. We found him in the burial chamber, pacing around the room. Standing in the entranceway, we watched him study a slanted aperture in one wall. It looked out upon a narrow slice of empty night sky. Then he walked to the pedestal that dominated the center of the room and inspected it again, trying to find the secret of the large alabaster block, the secret that would cause it to open and reveal a sarcophagus.

Apollo cleared his throat. Adama glanced up and his face lined with anger as he realized Baltar stood in the entranceway with us.

"I thought I ordered him removed to the *Galactica*," he said.

Apollo walked to his father and whispered to him, saying that he didn't choose to send Baltar back to the mother ship. Already the new warriors were responding to his insidious message, ignoring that it came from a suspected traitor.

"We don't dare expose Baltar to the Council,"

Apollo said, "not with their record of waffling on every important issue."

"I can handle the Council," Adama replied.

Then Baltar started in. We must follow his plan. We could drift forever looking for Earth, a planet that might after all just be the myth of half-drunken star voyagers. We should be aggressive—attack the Cylon capitol and seize power.

Adama scoffed, said Baltar couldn't be trusted, not any more. Realizing he was getting nowhere shouting at the commander's back, Baltar whined to us all that there was little time left.

I was so intent on all this that at first I didn't notice the change in the room. Light was beginning to flow into it. Apollo looked toward the slanted window and said that the star was pulsing again, glowing with more than double its ordinary light.

Because the aperture was so narrow, the new light seemed thick and sharply delineated. Adama, with a start, tersely muttered, "The light, that's it!" He strode to the other side of the chamber. Standing on a bench, he turned toward the window. Gradually the beam of light, which had been above his head, descended until it shined on his face, then his throat, then his chest. "It's true, I'm sure of it," Adama said. "That window was placed precisely where it is for a reason..."

Then the miracle happened. The light struck the medallion on Adama's chest. Immediately two different beams of light veered from its beveled surface toward the far corners of the room. Each bounced off the chests of two corner statues—tall statues of men dressed elaborately as sentinels—and rejoined in a splendid arc across the opposite wall, forming a blinding, dazzling light-triangle. A rumble vibrated the floor beneath us. My attention returned to the central pedestal, which Baltar pointed at wordlessly, his mouth hanging open.

Slowly, the top of the pedestal slid toward us. Cautiously we moved around the opening and found ourselves peering down long, steep stairs. Baltar leaped onto the stairway. Adama, stepping down from the bench, hollered at him to wait, but Baltar had disappeared into the darkness.

We followed.

The room below was richer and more decorated than the others. Each surface was delicately wrought in jewels. I had never seen such an array of gems and stones. Even in our dim torchlight, shimmering reflections bounced off them. There were deep red sapphires, the greenest emeralds I'd ever seen, diamonds. The room was positively cluttered with relics fashioned from gold, alabaster, pearls, lapis lazuli, faience, diorite. Layers of schist had broken away from the base of a statue and I tiptoed around them, afraid of splitting them further.

In the center of the room stood a massive sarcophagus. Bas-reliefs decorated its sides, depicting scenes of royal ceremony and noble domestic bliss. The oppressive smell that dominated the chamber seemed to waft out from it. I choked, longing for a breath of air that hadn't been sealed in a chamber for thousands of years.

"This must be it," Adama muttered. "The final resting place of Kobol's last Lord."

Baltar, jumping up from the other side of the sarcophagus, began struggling with its lid. Apollo grabbed at him, trying to break his grip, but Baltar succeeded in pushing aside the heavy stone slab with strength I would not have suspected, perhaps the strength of avarice. His eyes popped in wonder as he looked down into the sarcophagus. Apollo inhaled sharply. Adama, joining the two of them, examined the sarcophagus interior with tears welling in his eyes.

The last Lord lay in regal splendor, bright cerements in blue, red, and gold threads wrapped around him. If the mask that covered his shrouded head portrayed the last Lord, he must have been a handsome and impressive man in life. High-browed and slightly slant-eyed, with a thin nose and full lips, the mask suggested nobility, intelligence, and high purpose. In his right hand he held a scepter, the symbol of his power, no doubt. Embedded in the scepter's surface were large and glittering jewels.

Baltar put both of his hands upon the scepter and pulled at it roughly. He twisted it hard, apparently trying to break off the Lord's mummified hand at the wrist in order to get it.

"You dare to defy the holy crypt!" Adama shouted, as he seized Baltar by the shoulders and wrenched him backwards.

"Do you think I believe in all of that primitive superstition?" Baltar said, an ugly smile on his face.

I think Adama would have killed Baltar if the explosion that rocked the chamber hadn't sent us all crashing pell-mell to the floor. I fell beneath a tall, heavy statue of a queen or concubine. It rocked on its pedestal, as if to fall right on me, and I screamed. Apollo crawled over to me and pulled me out of range, but the statue did not fall.

I tried to ask Apollo what had happened but my voice was drowned out by another mighty rumble. This time a statue on the other side of the room did fall, remaining miraculously intact as it hit the stone flooring.

Gathering our wits together, we rushed up the stairs. Out of the corner of my eye I noticed Baltar momentarily lagging behind, his head turned back toward the resplendent sarcophagus.

I reached the top of the stairs just behind Apollo. The explosion had rocked the slab cover back into place, and Adama heaved against it with his shoulders and back. Apollo joined him, but their combined strength couldn't budge the slab.

Baltar scrambled by, pushing me aside with his hand, ramming me against the stairwell wall. He screamed that he wanted out, and ordered Adama and Apollo to stand aside. Shoving past Apollo, he started scratching at the underside of the slab, muttering that he had meant no harm. Apparently he believed the explosion was divine retribution, a result of his defiling the Lord's crypt. For the moment, that seemed a very real possibility. Baltar fell to his knees on a step. He implored Adama to help him to use the power in the medallion to get us all out. Adama merely shook his head and said quietly there was nothing he could do. Turning to Apollo, Adama asked him what he thought had happened.

"No question about it," Apollo said, bitterly. "The Cylons are attacking us out there, dropping heavy bombloads on our camp. And we're stuck in here—"

"Attack?" Baltar said. "Military attack? Then it's not the wrath of the—not the—punishing me."

He muttered incoherently for some time, while the rest of us tried to figure out what to do next. Adama and Apollo kept trying to move the stone slab. Perspiration streamed from their bodies. But the slab remained immobile. Finally, Apollo slumped to a sitting position on a stair, saying it was no use.

Baltar mumbled that he wanted nothing more in the universe than to get his hands on Lucifer. I asked him who Lucifer was, and why was he bringing him up now. Baltar ignored me and screamed at Adama to do something, save us. Another loud explosion made the entire tomb tremble. We scampered back to the burial chamber, expecting safety there. Sand sifted through cracks in the ceiling and walls. I moved into Apollo's arms.

Adama's eyes widened as he glimpsed something on a wall near the sarcophagus. He told Apollo to bring a torch closer. Its light fell on another stele, previously hidden by the now-fallen statue. In raised glyphs another message in the ancient language appeared.

Adama crouched by the lettering, oblivious to the frightening sounds of battle outside and threatening rumbles inside the tomb. He touched some of the symbols, saying they were familiar, but he couldn't translate the entire message. Apollo said there wasn't time for working out the meaning, we had to find a way out. His father merely knelt by the stele, puzzling over its words. More sand poured from the ceiling as the tomb seemingly took salvo after salvo from the attacking Cylons. Pieces of the wall fell away, crashed to the floor. Then Adama shouted victoriously:

"I've got it! That's it! Apollo, Serina, it's here, what we came for."

We peered over his shoulder. His face was so close to the stone stele that his head obscured its small glyphs. He pointed to a ribboned section at the bottom of the record. He said it was a record of the latter days, the final time on Kobol. It said something about the thirteenth tribe. The symbol for that tribe appeared throughout.

"We'll have to get a research team in here immediately," he shouted. "Experts who can discern the answers."

"Father, we have no time for that. We've got to get out of here!"

"But we must find out where they went."

The loudest explosion yet rocked the chamber. Cracks appeared in the wall above the stele. Another explosion and the cracks widened. The wall began to split apart and crumble. We reeled back and watched the stele bearing the message dissolve into fragments and fall to the floor, a collection of jagged shards. Adama rushed to them, picked up a couple of pieces as if he could put them together like a puzzle.

"The writings," he said, "we must preserve them."

"Father," Apollo said, gazing past Adama. "Look out there, beyond where the wall was."

We all looked. On the other side of the destroyed wall was a passageway, reaching toward darkness and shadow.

"Let's get out of here," Apollo begged, "while we've got the chance."

Adama didn't move an inch toward the new opening. I put a hand on his shouder and said quietly it was too late to recover the writings. They were gone, disintegrated, but in their destruction they'd provided a way out. The message had saved us.

Adama stood up and started toward the hole in the wall. Baltar's weak voice called to us from a debris-ridden corner of the room. He was pinned beneath a pair of fallen pillars.

Adama took charge and directed us as we alternatively tried to pull Baltar out from under the pillars. But we couldn't free him. The pillars were just too massive. Baltar was heavily pinioned.

"Our only chance, father," Apollo said, "is to leave him here now and send a team back for him. If there's time."

"*If there's time*?!" Baltar shouted, his voice sending echoes bouncing off every surface of the vast chamber. "You can't leave me here."

Adama stared at him and quietly replied there was no other choice. He promised Baltar to send the rescue team. Not satisfied with a promise, Baltar hurled curses first at Adama, then at all of us.

As we left the room and entered the dark, forbidding passageway, he started screaming about this Lucifer again, the most vile oaths and threats, saying he would tear Lucifer apart limb from limb, circuit by circuit, so help him. Circuit?, I thought, and made a mental note to investigate that matter further. *If* we ever get out of here. His last message to us was that we had not yet heard the last of Baltar. Adama whispered that the man would twist rhetoric until the very end of his life.

So—we've been exploring that passageway and others it led to. The battle, or whatever it is, continues outside the tomb, sending one loud rumble after another to shake the walls around us. This may be my last recording. I'm beginning to doubt we'll ever get out of here.

Apollo listened to the silence following the last part of the report on this crystal. Finally he realized there was nothing more recorded on it and, pressing a button, ejected it into his hand. He set it beside the other crystals he had played. They were lined up in a neat row on a writing table. There were no more. He rubbed his forehead, tried to think. What to do now? He returned to the drawer where he had originally found the recording crystals, rummaged around in it for a long time, hoping—praying to find one more there. But he knew there were no more.

CHAPTER NINETEEN

First the Kobol star briefly flared, then a wall of Cylon fighters obscured the momentary brightness. For a long moment they hovered there, as if advertising the enormous dimensions of their threat, then they began peeling off from the dense formation. In graceful, menacing sweeps and arcs they began forming into the pinwheel assault.

Starbuck realized they would break away from the pinwheel to initiate strafing and bombing runs. There was no time to lose. Ordering one group of warriors back to the shuttle on the double, he started running down the dead city's stone causeway, shouting Apollo's name. Cylon fighters started sweeping down on the camp, laying down a steady line of laser fire. A couple of bombs hit tents dead center and flames ripped them open. Another contingent of attackers swept down and more tents burst into flame.

Athena, closely followed by Gemi, raced up to him. Their bodies were darkly outlined in shadow by the bright fires burning out of control behind them.

"Where's Apollo and Serina?" he shouted to her. "Where's the Commander?"

"Last I saw, they were taking Baltar into the tomb."

He looked toward the pyramid just in time to see a Cylon ship aim a bomb at its northern face. The drop was a shade off target and only sent an eruption of stone chips into the air. Smoke from a direct hit curled up from a far face of the pyramid.

"Better get back to your viper, Lieutenant," Athena hollered.

Starbuck hesitated, wanting to run to the pyramid, look for Apollo and the others.

"But—we can't leave them. We've got to—I mean, they'll blow that thing to pieces."

"It'd waste time to go look for them. We've got to knock those dirty creeps out of the sky—now! But do what you want, I'm going to—"

"No, you look for them. I'll—"

"Stow that, Starbuck! I'm going up! Everybody from the class is ready and we're going."

"Are you crazy? Some of those guys can barely fly, they might shoot each other down."

Athena glared at him, then said in a low voice that was almost as menacing as the Cylon raid:

"You do what you want, Lieutenant, but I'm gone. Goodbye."

She started running toward the viper landing area. Gemi, glancing around unsurely for a moment, hesitated, touched Starbuck briefly on the arm, then scampered after Athena.

"Lord help us," Starbuck muttered, then set off after them.

Whenever he had been ill, Boomer had always found recuperation infinitely worse than the disease itself. At the height of sickness, he accepted his incapacity as a rule of the universe and was able to remain still without any tension. But, during recuperative periods, he always felt nervous, ready to go. He would drift off into dreams in which he was back in his cockpit, aiming his laser gun at a point halfway between two lines of fire coming at him. Lying still became a physical impossibility. He discovered hundreds of ways to move his body, shift about, find metal pieces of his bed to touch, twist his neck to look at an area of the sick bay ceiling whose topography he'd already memorized.

He did not even want to be cared for any more. He had told Cassiopeia several times to pay more attention to the others, who no doubt needed her ministrations more than he did. She always replied that all her charges were equal to her, and that he should stop pulling rank.

When news of the Cylon raid on the Kobol landing party had spread through the *Galactica*, messengers continued to rush into sick bay with each new bulletin. Boomer could take his inaction no longer. Straining every muscle, he pulled himself out of his bed and, with great effort, planted both feet upon the floor. Standing up, he felt a wave of dizziness, a blast in his mind like the weakness he had experienced when the disease had first struck him. Gritting his teeth, he concentrated on clearing his mind of confusing images and drawing on his viper jumpsuit. As he zipped the final zipper, Cassiopeia came running into the room.

"You're not going anywhere, warrior," she shouted.

He almost wanted to say, You're right, I'm not going anywhere, but instead he shook his head negatively at her and said:

"No time to argue. I'm going to the command bridge. No, Cassiopeia, don't say it."

"You lunatics," she muttered.

"Lunatics?"

"Yes. You and Jolly and Greenbean and Giles, all of you. Looneys. Everybody in sick bay is trying to stagger out of it right now. Where are you going, Boomer?"

His voice was weak, but firm:

"I'm assembling my squadron."

As he came onto the bridge, Boomer heard Rigel telling Tigh:

"The Cylon fighters are pressing the attack, taking the advantage again."

"And we don't have sufficient warrior personnel to—"

"Yes, you do!" Boomer shouted, his voice not betraying any sign of the weakness he still felt.

Tigh whirled around and his jaw seemed to drop a foot when he saw Boomer, flanked by Jolly and Greenbean, the rest of the former invalids grouped behind them.

"What is this?" Tigh said.

"Colonel," Boomer said, "Blue Squadron, reporting for duty."

Tigh walked to them, his smile affectionate.

"Lieutenant," he said softly, "you obviously can't even stand."

Boomer knew he had the edge now. He just smiled and replied:

"A viper's flown from the sitting position, sir."

Tigh glared at Boomer, but the lieutenant had won his point. He almost fell from exhaustion when Tigh ordered that all launch bays be made ready for Blue Squadron.

"Fly in pairs," Starbuck ordered over the open commline. "Stick to your leaders, protect them! We may have a chance."

He closed off the commline and muttered:

"One chance in a hundred."

Dietra's voice, full of a sturdy confidence, broadcast to all:

"Starbuck, we'll ionize them!"

They're still in the mock-flight rooms, Starbuck thought. One success in battle and they think they're indestructible. Don't they realize that previously they had only to contend with the surprised protectors of a single launch pod, and now they're up against a full Cylon task force? Hell, maybe they shouldn't realize that. If you laugh at the enemy, at least you go out in style—that was the warriors' slogan, anyway.

At least the squadron had been able to launch without any enemy interference. Starbuck figured that was just another burst of the luck he was famous for. Some luck, he thought. Here I've been beaten in battle, captured and taken to a Cylon base-star, and returned here just in time to lead raw troops against a whole task force of Cylon spacecraft. That's luck, all right.

They were still climbing off the planet when some Cylon ships veered away from the attack on the ground camp and rushed toward the assembling squadron of vipers.

"They've seen us," Starbuck yelled.

He leveled his viper and ordered the squadron to come to combat status.

"Look at all of them," Athena said. "How many are there? Looks like eighty, ninety, a hundred—"

"Athena!" Starbuck shouted. "You're not on the bridge. Quit counting!"

"You afraid of the odds, Lieutenant?"

"Stop prodding me and let's see how you can shoot...darling."

"You got it...sir."

A moment later the sky was a tangled muddle of battling airships. The inexperience of his troops was working to their advantage, Starbuck realized. The pilots of the Cylon craft expected certain flight maneuvers, tactics, the trainees hadn't even been taught yet. This edge allowed the cadet pilots to squirm out from under attack and blast Cylon ships to smithereens by coming up at them bellyside. Vipers whirled and weaved around their attackers insidiously. Cylon pilot after Cylon pilot was caught by surprise.

Starbuck began to believe their chances were better than he'd thought, then Athena's voice ruined his brief, newfound confidence.

"Starbuck! It's Gemi. Little Gemi. She's hit, highside. Now another's coming at her. Oh, God, they got her. She's gone, Starbuck, gone."

He tried to remember which one was Gemi, could not quite place her. But he had precious little time to try to remember. The sound of Athena's crying over the commline was jarring.

"Okay, Athena, okay. Stay in control."

"I'm *in* control, damn you. Don't worry about me."

He had no time to argue. Two Cylon warships were bearing down on him. With a quick burst of laser fire, a slide to the left, and another shot from his laser, he transformed the enemy vessels into two blazing fireballs settling down onto the desert surface of Kobol.

"Hit 'em and roll away," he shouted to the squadron.

The air was filled with fire and the thousands of pieces of shattered craft.

"Brie," called Dietra, "one on your tail."

Starbuck tensed. Brie had not shown much skill during training, her shots always just off target, her control of her ship just a bit erratic. Would she blow it this time, become another casualty like what-was-her-name, Gemi?

"Breaking," Brie screamed.

She put her viper into a reverse loop. The Cylon raider flashed by beneath her. She came down on his tail and, lasers blazing, blasted him to oblivion. As it burst into flame, both Brie and Dietra whooped for joy.

In another quarter, Athena bore down on a Cylon warship and blew it apart.

"Nice going, Athena," Starbuck hollered.

"I think that was the one that got Gemi, the dirty—"

She could not complete the curse as she came under fire from a pair of new attackers. Disposing of one with a quick blast, she evaded the other momentarily, before it dived up at her.

"It's hopeless, Starbuck," she shouted.

Hopeless or not, she got the drop on this one, too, firing her laser instinctively, achieving a direct hit on the cockpit.

Starbuck would have congratulated her again, but he had to go to Dietra's aid. Hurtling down on a Cylon ship that was hot in pursuit of her viper, Starbuck nailed him just in time, just before he would have destroyed her with a shattering fusillade. Dietra breathed a sharp sigh of relief before saying:

"Thanks, Starbuck."

"Don't mention it."

"That's the last time."

He laughed as he pulled his joystick toward him and rose above her. It was hard now to discern anything through the clouds of smoke and the rain of battle. A brief glance downward at the camp told Starbuck that most of it was in flames. People moved down there, however—insects scurrying from their potential exterminators.

"Starbuck!" Athena yelled. "Watch it!"

Suddenly he was surrounded by Cylons. It was a pinwheel attack. He put his viper into a spin, the best way to break out of the pinwheel. But, he sensed, he was a moment too late to make it.

Once inside his cockpit, Boomer felt much better. It was as if the last remaining vestiges of his malady had been left behind in his flight locker. He began to feel confident. Even the omens seemed to be in his favor. Jenny, the flight crew leader who acted tough and scorned all advances, had kissed Boomer for luck. He wondered if she'd be that friendly to him when he returned. He doubted it.

Rigel's voice gave the final rundown:

"Two pilots definitely unable to launch. Unconscious in their cockpits."

Boomer smiled. Only two. That was a good omen, too. Nearly everybody who'd been down sick had found the strength to return to combat.

"Launch vipers!" Tigh bellowed.

"Transferring launch control," Rigel's steady voice declared. "Launch when ready."

"Launching!" Boomer cried.

Thrust back against his seat and neck brace, Boomer found himself on the verge of blanking out as his ship zoomed down launch tube. He cleared his mind as his ship cleared the other shell of the *Galactica*. As he flew his viper into formation, he found he had a tough time controlling it, but somehow he managed it. Style and class were okay, but doing it was better.

The outer squadron ships joined him in formation and he punched out the coordinates for their flight plan. He hoped they were not too late for the battle. If the Cylons had the advantage when they arrived, his beleaguered squadron of semi-invalids could not go it alone. As he performed the necessary checkout of all his systems he noticed that both his coordination and alertness were improving rapidly. It felt like old times. He eased his joystick forward.

"Are you all right, Boomer?"

It was the familiar voice of Colonel Tigh.

"I copy, *Galactica*. Jolly?"

"In your wake."

"Then let's go!"

Above Kobol, Boomer quickly punched up his scanner for close-range survey and located the area of combat. The Galactican forces were holding their own. If anything, they had the advantage. But how long could inexperienced pilots hold off an entire Cylon task force? Already it appeared that one viper was trapped in a Cylon pinwheel maneuver.

Time to go in.

"There they are! Blue Squadron, let's join the party."

Boomer was amazed at just how good he really felt.

"I'm in trouble!" Starbuck shouted, when he realized that the spin would not slip him free of the

pinwheel. Although he hadn't caught a serious hit
yet, laser fire was scarring the superstructure of his
viper.

"Hang on, Starbuck," Athena responded. "I'm
coming in!"

Great, he thought, *the hotshot pilot's going to
demonstrate her skill again. I'm done for. Why
didn't I memorize one of Boxey's prayers before—*

In front of him a Cylon vessel disintegrated.
Then another one burst into flame. He was able to
blast a third and fourth ship himself. As the other
Cylons made a wise retreat, Starbuck realized that
the pinwheel was broken. The smoke cleared, and
he saw Athena's viper flashing by. She had done it,
she had bagged the first two ships and saved his
bacon.

"I'm still alive," he whispered, incredulous. He
almost clapped a hand over his mouth, fearful that
his whisper had been transmitted over the commline.

"You all right, Starbuck?" Athena hollered.

"Fine. Ah...thanks, Athena."

"Four more to port...engaging!"

He was impressed by the down-to-business
certainty in her voice. He would have to remember
to credit her valor in any report he made of this
battle. If he ever got a chance to make a report. Hell,
not just *her* name. The names of *all* of them. His
makeshift combat squadron was really proving its
skill today.

However, even though they had suffered few
casualties and had taken out so many of their
enemy, they were still outnumbered. Should he
order a retreat? Where to? Back on the ground, they
would be strafed to a finish. If they returned to the
Galactica, they would be putting the mother ship in
extreme jeopardy. They could not *go* anywhere,

Starbuck realized. Their only chance was to stay and fight.

As if reading his mind, Dietra suddenly shouted:

"We're trapped."

Starbuck replied grimly:

"Let's go out fighting. Athena!"

"On your wing, Starbuck."

"Good. Just wanted to know where you were. Might need help again."

"With you, Lieutenant."

"Regroup above the pyramid. Go into star formations. Then we'll attack!"

As they all headed for the skies above the pyramid, Dietra yelled:

"Let's mow 'em down, cadets!"

Hovering in formation, Starbuck was just about to order the attack to begin when he saw the growing dots behind the Cylon forces. They were vipers! Materializing out of nowhere. All squadrons were down except the one with the landing party. Where did these vipers come from? He thought of the pilots in sick bay and how weak they had all looked on his last visit. He could not believe his ears when he heard Boomer's voice over his commline:

"The mop-up brigade's here, Starbuck. You want to help or just sit this one out?"

Starbuck could not help laughing.

"But . . . but you can't fly a viper, Boomer. You're in—"

"Neither can you, Chucklehead. I saw you getting your butt saved from that pinwheel. *Slop-py*!, bucko."

Starbuck continued to laugh heartily as he ordered his cadet squadron to move forward.

Tigh wished he could be flying right along with his squadrons. He had often asked Adama to be restored to combat status, but the commander always dismissed the idea, saying he was required on the bridge. Being on the bridge ... sometimes he hated the bridge. Bridge duty meant standing by monitors and watching the massacre of men and women whom you had come to love and respect. He never could quite accept the helplessness of being outside any battle.

Omega's voice interrupted his thoughts:

"Colonel, come here, please."

Tigh rushed to communications section, fully expecting the worst.

"Combat report coming in," Omega announced. His face reflected sudden surprise as he read the words on the screen. "Surprise factor is total. Cylons running. Shall we pursue? Boomer."

Tigh could not help smiling. The battle had been won, by some rapidly trained cadets and a bunch of patients fresh off their sickbeds. That should show the gloom-and-doom soothsayers who said that *Galactica* could not succeed, that the odds against it spelled out defeat. If we can knock out a Cylon task force with these troops, we can do anything! Tigh felt elated. He looked at Omega, who was still awaiting a response to Boomer's coded message.

"Negative to Boomer's request to pursue. Bring them home. Any word from the commander or Apollo?"

"No, sir. Last message said they'd been last seen going into the tomb."

Tigh turned away, his joy suddenly sabotaged by worry. Was that to be the punchline—a victory followed by the loss of Adama and Apollo? It couldn't be!

CHAPTER TWENTY

Apollo held the recorder in his hands, one thumb
tentatively fingering the defective button. Serina
would have wanted him to add to her history,
complete the record she was making. But he could
not do that right now, not with all the events so fresh
and painful in his mind. He was not a newsman, he
had no taste for history. Perhaps later, when he had
time to be reflective. But not now.

Shutting his eyes tightly to hold back another
outbreak of tears, he began to see images of Serina
form, disintegrate, and reform among the elusive
dots and lines that swam on the inside of his eyelids.

—Serina emerging from a group of scarred and
dirty Caprican survivors, pleading for an explanation of the destruction all around them. He had
recognized her from the video tape he'd viewed of

her reporting the Caprican disaster as it happened.

—Serina rushing at him in a corridor of the corruptly governed luxury liner *Rising Star.* (In those early times she'd always seemed to come at him out of shadow.)

—Serina smiling gratefully when Apollo surprised Boxey with an android version of his lost daggit.

—Serina looking at him with love in her eyes after an embrace.

—Serina furious with him, acting really feisty over a matter of disputed ethics.

—Serina crying joyfully at the sealing ceremony.

—Serina taunting him for not believing she could ever pilot a viper.

—Serina falling in the middle of that ancient city street.

He wanted to halt the rush of these memories, put some organization to them, try to discover some sense in what had happened.

After a long and arduous journey through the tomb's complex catacombs, they had finally found the way out. Adama, still saddened by the destruction of the stele about the thirteenth tribe, led the way. They emerged into a scene of dying fire and debris-strewn air. The colonnade which led to the tomb had miraculously escaped the ravages of attack, but the camp and much of the ancient city had been devastated.

"The camp's been obliterated," Apollo shouted back to Serina and Adama. "Everybody's gone."

"Maybe they got away then," Serina said.

"I hope so."

Tired and exhausted, they trod toward the remains of the camp. Sand, stirred up by the Cylon onslaught, settled in layers upon their clothing. Behind him, Apollo heard Serina cry:

"Starbuck!"

Whirling around, he saw Starbuck standing by a partially demolished pillar. Next to him stood Athena, Dietra, Brie, and other *Galactica* warriors. They looked terrible, their faces weary and haggard.

"What happened?" Apollo said, rushing to Starbuck.

Starbuck looked skyward, his eyes rueful.

"We lost some good pilots up there."

Athena broke away from the group and joined her father. She buried her head in his shoulder and began to sob.

"I heard from Colonel Tigh," Starbuck said. His voice was soft, serious, laconic. "He said he'd like us off the surface and underway as soon as possible. He's anticipating reinforcements from the Cylons, a new attack."

"He's right," Adama said, the first words he'd spoken since they'd left the tomb. "Let's leave the surface as quickly as possible. Assemble everyone at the shuttle. The shuttle is still functioning, is it not?"

"They didn't score a hit on it, sir."

"A small consolation, but we can give thanks."

Starbuck suggested that some of the warriors make a final survey of the camp to see if there were any more survivors.

"Everybody we found is at the shuttle already," he said. "Be careful. One of our pilots observed a couple of Cylon ships who weren't part of the attack force land in an area beyond the pyramid. Keep a sharp lookout, just in case it's true. Some of those red lights may be wandering around here someplace."

After the search party went off, Adama ordered the rest of them to proceed to the shuttle. They all tried to walk fast, but events had taken their toll. Apollo felt a desperate urge to sleepwalk all the way.

Starbuck, his voice raspy with exhaustion, muttered to himself:

"Can't say I'll miss this place. Would've liked a chance to look around a bit and—Apollo!"

Apollo spun around, alerted by the shift in Starbuck's voice from weariness to agitation. The red lights on their helmets shining, catching pieces of sand and debris still floating in the air, two Cylon warriors lumbered toward them, laser rifles held in their thick arms and—abruptly—firing. Apollo moved sideways, and heard the sizzle of the laser beam striking a pillar next to him. Bits of stone fell around his head. Drawing his pistol, he returned fire. To his left Starbuck had already started shooting. The ambushers disappeared behind a pile of stone blocks.

Apollo gestured the rest of the group to cover while he and Starbuck edged forward, from one heap of rubble to another.

"I can get a better angle from that rise over there," Starbuck said. "Cover me."

As soon as he stuck his head above the rubble pile, a beam of laser fire buzzed by him.

"I think they're suggesting I take the long way round."

Apollo eased toward the side of the rubble heap to lay down a barrage of cover fire for Starbuck's maneuver. The lieutenant was halfway across the street when a Cylon appeared from behind the triangular remains of a building corner and took a bead on him. Starbuck tried to dodge and caught his foot in a crack in the roadway. He fell heavily, his face grimacing in pain. Apollo quickly dropped the Cylon before he could get off another shot at the helpless warrior.

"I've done something to my ankle," Starbuck shouted.

"Wait, I'll be right there," Apollo said.

He was almost at Starbuck's side when Serina screamed:

"No, Apollo. Look out! The roof."

He felt laser heat nearly singeing his chest as he pivoted and saw a flash of metal—his enemy ducking beneath the cover afforded by a roof overhang.

"Can you crawl?" he said to Starbuck.

"I'll do my best."

Crouching, Apollo kept a watchful eye on the roof as Starbuck pulled himself up to all fours and began to crawl toward the nearest intact building. Serina came running out from her hiding place in a doorway, her gun drawn.

"Go back, Serina," Apollo yelled.

"No! You guys need all the protection you can get."

Serina joined him and took up position on the other side of Starbuck, who continued to move forward, dragging his hurt ankle. At the same time, Athena made her way to the pile of rubble and fanned her pistol toward the perimeter. In the silence the only sound was Starbuck crawling.

"This is too slow," Starbuck muttered. "The pain's gone down. I think I can limp the rest of the way. Help me up."

Serina offered her free arm and Starbuck pulled himself to his feet. Although he could barely put pressure on his left leg he moved it anyway, wincing with his first step.

"Let Apollo support you," Serina said. Starbuck put his arm on Apollo's shoulder and the captain bore his weight. They had almost reached the building when Athena started shooting. Four new Cylons had suddenly materialized near the colonnade. Beyond them was an incongruous robotlike figure, shadowy in the distance. It seemed to wear a red robe and have a different kind of light in its headgear. Laser fire erupted simultaneously from the weapons of the four Cylons.

"Get him inside," Serina shouted, turning toward the new ambushers. "I'll cover."

Apollo hesitated, intending to order her to take care of Starbuck while he took on the attackers, but there was no time to switch. He hefted Starbuck through the building's dark doorway, propped him against a wall, then returned to the street. Serina crouched behind a fallen pillar. He ran to her side, fell down beside her.

"Got one," she muttered without looking at him. "Impressed?"

"You stay out of sight. My turn now."

"Don't play hero. We'll do this together, all of us. Nobody gets to retreat. By the way, I love you."

"What a time to—"

"Shut up and—oh my God! Look out!"

She pointed her pistol over his shoulder and shot. The Cylon who'd tried to shoot them in the back spun around, sparks flying from the wide crease her shot had caused in his metal battlesuit. The creature was not disabled. After it regained its balance it kept on coming, firing a blast that just missed both of them.

Serina fired again. This time the Cylon fell, with a resounding thump, to the ground.

"One more Cylon warrior sent to his—oh!"

Her cry was small, as if just a twinge of pain, but she arched her back and went limp, falling sideways across the pillar.

"Serina," Apollo cried. "Serina!"

She smiled up at him briefly, then her eyes glazed over and closed. She was unconscious.

Angrily Apollo started firing wildly. His bursts

allowed Athena to scramble forward and add her own well-aimed shots. The two of them, brother and sister, stood on either side of the street, blasting away at any sign of metal, any hint of Cylon. It was a proper shootout, and a wild one. Suddenly Apollo was conscious of Starbuck yelling:

"Hey! Stop! They're dead. All of them."

Apollo dropped his pistol to his side and looked ahead, where the remaining Cylon warriors did indeed lie dead in the roadway. But it was not, as Starbuck had said, all of them. The mysterious robotlike figure, its strange lights dimming, faded into the shadows and vanished. Normally, Apollo might have pursued him, or it, but now he could only fall to his knees and embrace his limp, unconscious wife.

Back on the *Galactica*, time seemed to speed up. Things happened too quickly. Even now, Apollo's memory could not assimilate all the events, all the details.

He remembered waiting outside the entrance to the life station. Boomer and Tigh paced the corridor, while Starbuck, his ankle heavily bandaged, leaned against a wall and tried to comfort Apollo.

The door opened. Cassiopeia came out, tears sparkling her eyes.

"It's going to be all right," Starbuck said, getting to Cassiopeia before Apollo, in spite of his game leg. "Isn't it?"

Cassiopeia buried her head in Starbuck's chest. Apollo started to run to the life station door, when his father, coming along the corridor with Boxey in his arms, yelled:

"Wait!"

Apollo halted at the door, glared at his father.

"It's my right," he said. "I've got to be with her."

"You will, I promise you. But give Dr. Salik every chance."

Boxey, incongruously, was smiling. Of course, nobody had wanted to tell him how serious his mother's condition was. Apollo felt he should tell the boy immediately, but the words stuck in his throat. Starbuck whispered something in Cassiopeia's ear, probably asking her to look cheerful, since she turned toward Apollo with a forced smile on her face.

"Hi, Starbuck," Boxey said, leaping down from Adama's arms. "I heard you did good."

"Well, ah, you know how it is. When you're great, you're great."

"I want to hear all about it after I see Mother."

Starbuck struggled to stay smiling. Apollo was about to embrace Boxey when Dr. Salik opened the life station door and said it was okay to go in now. His eyes betrayed no clue to Serina's condition.

Apollo shoved past the doctor and hurried to Serina's side. Her eyes were closed, her face expressionless. *It's too late*, he thought. Then her eyes opened and she smiled weakly.

"Hello, darling," she said. "I shouldn't have stopped to gloat over my kill, should I?"

"Oh, Serina, I—"

"I love you."

"Mama," Boxey screamed. He was afraid. He'd learned the truth without anyone telling him. He ran to Serina's bed, had to climb up on the railing around it in order to look at her properly.

"Boxey!" Serina said. "I'm so glad to see you."

Her voice is so weak, Apollo thought. *It seems to come from far away.*

"I hear you won the whole war," Boxey said.

"Well, I had a little help," Serina said, smiling

and touching the boy's cheek. The effort cost her dearly and she dropped her hand suddenly. For a moment life seemed to go out of her eyes.

"Serina," Apollo said, a desperate effort to call her back. It worked, for her eyes came alive again.

"Mama," Boxey said, his voice tearful. "You're going away, aren't you?"

Apollo did not know what to do. He wanted to hold Boxey close, continue to protect him from the truth.

"Yes, Boxey," Serina answered. "I am. But your father will take care of you."

As she said this, she hugged Boxey tightly, as if she didn't ever want to let him go.

"And I'll love you always," she whispered. "You won't forget that, will you?"

Boxey finally could hold back his tears no longer. He said he wouldn't forget. Releasing him a little, she wiped his eyes, saying:

"Is that any way for a junior warrior to act?" Boxey struggled to control his crying, succeeded. "That's better. Much better."

Adama walked up behind Boxey and gently took the boy into his arms. Boxey smiled down at Serina, who said again, "That's better."

After Adama had taken the boy out of the room, Serina said:

"I shouldn't have done that."

Her words confused Apollo.

"Done what?"

"Told him to stop crying, act like a junior warrior. The worst of the so-called male virtues. A grown man doesn't cry and all that. But—but I couldn't stand watching him. I—"

"Take it easy, dear. It's all right."

Now she began to cry.

"No, it isn't all right. It isn't fair. It isn't fair to you."

"To me? If I could trade places—"

She put a hand over his mouth and, with a struggle, stemmed the flow of her own tears.

"I understand," she said. "But I want you to know I feel very, very lucky. Even if all we had was a brief time, it will be—"

"We'll have more time together."

She laughed weakly.

"Please don't, Apollo. You don't believe that. It's only a matter—"

"I do. You've convinced me. A spirit like yours can't end."

Her eyes began to tear up again.

"Oh, that's all right then. I can accept—accept the spirit idea, thank you."

Then a pain surged through her body and she stiffened. She pulled Apollo close.

"I love you," she whispered.

"I love you," he responded, but never knew if she heard him.

He picked up a recording crystal, the earliest, the first one he'd listened to—so long ago now, it seemed. He considered replaying it, hearing her voice again, but realized he could not do that, not now. Carefully, delicately, he replaced all the crystals in the drawer where he'd originally found them.

Somebody had piled her combat outfit on their bed. He had picked it up to fold it away when something fell out of the pocket of her flight jacket—an odd, jagged object. Examining it, he saw it was a potsherd, a piece of what might have been a vase or jar. She must have found it down on Kobol and pocketed it as a souvenir. Holding it now, he became afraid it might break, and he set it on a nearby table with extreme care.

Somebody knocked gently on the compartment door.

"Who is it?"

"Just me. Starbuck."

"What do you want?"

"Somebody here to talk with you."

"I don't want to talk with anybody just—"

"All right then, somebody here who needs you. Open up, damn it."

He opened the door and saw Boxey standing meekly beside Starbuck. The boy looked miserable. Apollo gathered him in his arms and embraced him.

"I'll be down at the . . . I'll be somewhere, if you need me," Starbuck said, and limped down the corridor without waiting for an answer.

Apollo led Boxey into the room. The boy glanced around, his eyes glistening, then he muttered:

"I didn't want her to go."

"I know. But it's her body that's gone, Boxey. Not her spirit or her love for us. We'll have that always."

Boxey nodded slowly. Apollo looked into his eyes. Could he care for this boy? Could he follow Serina's implicit orders and become his father? It didn't seem possible, it'd be too big a responsibility. In his head he could hear his own father telling him there was no responsibility he couldn't handle. Well, maybe he could, maybe he couldn't—the point was, he *had* to.

Boxey kept rubbing the back of his hand against his tear-streaked eyes.

"I guess . . ." he said. "I guess I won't make a very good warrior."

Apollo remembered Serina's regret at telling the

boy that junior warriors shouldn't cry. He hugged the boy close and whispered:

"Son, you'll make a fine warrior. But let's hope you never have to be one. Let's hope—" He stopped talking, held him for a long time, then released him and took his hand. "C'mon, there's a lot to do. Let's go."

Before he closed the door to the compartment, as he thought he saw Serina standing in the shadows, smiling, a shudder went through his body. It was his imagination, of course, but he preferred not to turn on a light to verify that.

EPILOGUE

Lucifer stayed in the shadows, crouching behind a colonnade pillar, for a long while—until he was certain all the humans had shuttled off the planet. He knew it was imperative that he act eventually. The power pack that he had inserted into his chest to enable him to function at this distance from his main units could easily malfunction under such dangerous alien conditions.

It might have been a mistake to travel to the planet himself, an act of illogical bravado accompanying his temporary mania for leadership. He had used the fierce combat in the Kobol skies as a shield for his ship's descent. The portions of his programming that demanded loyalty to Baltar had impelled him to attempt a rescue of the man. It had not seemed a foolish idea at the time, since his task force had clearly been winning the battle. From the abandoned city he had watched the tide turn as the second contingent of colonial vipers had entered the fray. Those humans, whatever their repulsive traits, could certainly fight their way out of a trap against incredible odds. Lucifer could almost admire them. Perhaps the whole race was like Starbuck, a trifle overbearing but clever, amusing, and resourceful. Imagining a whole race of Starbucks, he wondered briefly if he were on the wrong side. However, a fail-safe mechanism clicked in and countered the wayward thought. His allegiance to the Cylon Empire could not be removed without an extensive program restructuring.

Lucifer regretted that Starbuck had been a member of the group who had wiped out his honor guard. A cheerless reunion, not what he had anticipated. All four warriors who had formed the guard lay dead within Lucifer's view. They looked gray, as if the metal of their battle suits had dimmed when they died. What would have happened, Lucifer wondered, if the humans had elected to ferret him out? His linkup to his main units could be stretched just so thin. If the fleet captured him and took him out of range of his base-star, would the break in the linkup send him haywire—would he act like a human suddenly insane? He did not care to speculate on the possibilities.

Time to look for Baltar. Lucifer came out from behind the pillar, the lights of his body and head now restored to full power, now that the threat of attack was diminished.

Signals from a sensor that he had planted on Baltar showed that the human was somewhere in the depths of the vast pyramidal tomb. Not the best place to have to search for anyone, Lucifer thought. As he worked his way through the labyrinths, his memory banks mapping the route, he sensed his power pack straining to function inside the pyramid's thick walls. Just when he thought he might have to abandon the search, he found his quarry. Baltar lay under two crossed pillars, his eyes shut, sleeping quite peacefully. Lucifer shook him awake.

"Lucifer! What in blazes are you doing here?"

"Rescuing you, it seems. Again."

"I'm trapped. Hurt. Get me out of here, immediately."

"By your command."

Activating a stress counterbalance in his arms which allowed him to triple his normal lifting powers, Lucifer easily moved the two pillars off Baltar's legs. Baltar gaped down at his freed limbs, his eyes fearful.

"I—I may never walk again," he whimpered.

Lucifer gave the legs a quick med-scan.

"Your ambulatory abilities will not be hampered. A couple of broken bones, that's all, easy to mend. When we return to base ship, I'll be able to meld them together in no time."

"Return to base ship? How do you propose to do that? Float me out of this lousy tomb?"

"I will carry you."

"How noble of you."

"Yes. We may be able to turn it into legend. Maybe not. . . . Legend is easier to formulate when you win the battle."

"You—you lost?"

"It seems so."

"I want to talk to you about the attack when we get back. How dare you launch fighters without my express orders?"

"An aberration, I'm afraid. A malfunction. A touch of the human disease."

"The human disease?"

"I began to believe I could outthink anyone. I will need to make a systematic analysis of my behavior during your absence. I must discover where I went wrong."

"Don't worry. I'll show you."

"Yes, I'm sure you will."

"Lucifer, when I get through with you, your name will be mud. Your *secret* name will be mud."

"Close, but not right. Please, arch your back so I may lift you."

"Can you carry the weight?"

"I can carry any weight without feeling it. It's mass that gives me trouble. Fortunately, I made you diet."

"Torture, that was—hey, careful. Ouch! Take it easy. I'm not comfortable like this."

"I cannot carry you any other way. It's only a short distance, after we leave the tomb, to my ship."

Lucifer lugged Baltar through the many corridors, paying scant attention to the man's grunts, complaints, and groans of displeasure.

Back on the base ship, after Lucifer had attended to Baltar's injuries, the man regained some of his jauntiness.

"We could make quite a team, Lucifer," he said, smiling that annoying smile.

Lucifer resisted his programming and remained silent. He did not wish to consider teaming with Baltar. He was, as a subordinate officer on the *Galactica* might have put it, looking for a way to snag a transfer off this rattletrap.

The greatest space epic ever!

BattlestaR GALACTICA

BATTLESTAR GALACTICA...a gripping
interstellar adventure...a triumphant TV
spectacular...a major new film from
Universal! Available from Berkley at your local
bookstore or use this handy coupon for
ordering.

___BATTLESTAR GALACTICA (03958-7)
@ $1.95
by Glen A. Larson and Robert Thurston

___BATTLESTAR GALACTICA 2: THE CYLON
DEATH MACHINE (04080-1) @ $1.95
by Glen A. Larson and Robert Thurston

___BATTLESTAR GALACTICA 3: THE TOMBS OF
KOBOL (04267-7) @ $1.95
by Glen A. Larson and Robert Thurston

___BATTLESTAR GALACTICA:
THE PHOTOSTORY (04139-5) @ $2.50
by Glen A. Larson; Edited and Adapted by
Richard Anobile

Berkley Book Mailing Service
P.O. Box 690
Rockville Centre, NY 11570

Please send me the above titles. I am enclosing $___
(Please add 50¢ per copy to cover postage and handling). Send check or
money order—no cash or C.O.D.'s. Allow three weeks for delivery.

NAME___

ADDRESS___

CITY___ STATE/ZIP___

#14

New Bestsellers from Berkley...
The best in paperback reading!

___ **BY THE RIVERS OF BABYLON** (04431-9—$2.75)
Nelson De Mille

___ **THE LAST CONVERTIBLE** (04034-8—$2.50)
Anton Myrer

___ **THE LEGACY** (04183-2—$2.25)
John Coyne, based on a story by Jimmy Sangster

___ **LINKS** (04048-8—$2.25)
Charles Panati

___ **LEAH'S JOURNEY** (04430-0—$2.50)
Gloria Goldreich

___ **THE SINS OF RACHEL ELLIS** (04144-1—$2.25)
Philip Caveney

___ **STAR SIGNS FOR LOVERS** (04238-3—$2.50)
Robert Worth

___ **THE TANGENT FACTOR** (04120-4—$2.25)
Lawrence Sanders

___ **A TIME FOR TRUTH** (04185-9—$2.50)
William E. Simon

___ **THE VISITOR** (04210-3—$2.50)
Jere Cunningham

Available at your local bookstore or return this form to:

**Berkley Book Mailing Service
P.O. Box 690
Rockville Centre, NY 11570**

Please send me the books I have checked above. I am enclosing $_____ (please add 50¢ to cover postage and handling).
Send check or money order—no cash or C.O.D.'s please.

Name _____

Address_____

City_____ State/Zip_____

Please allow three weeks for delivery.

1